Swimming Cat Cove

THE 2ND ALLISON O'NEIL MYSTERY

LAUREN WRIGHT DOUGLAS

THE NAIAD PRESS, INC.
1997

Printed in the United States of America on acid-free paper
First Edition

Editor: Christine Cassidy
Cover designer: Bonnie Liss (Phoenix Graphics)
Typesetter: Sandi Stancil

Library of Congress Cataloging-in-Publication Data

Douglas, Lauren Wright, 1947 –
    Swimming cat cove : an Allison O'Neil mystery / Lauren Wright
Douglas.
        p.   cm.
    ISBN 1-56280-168-6 (alk. paper)
    1. Lesbians—Fiction.   I. Title.
PS3554.08263S9   1997
813'.54—dc21   96-45477
                                                                                      CIP

"Call the cops," Kerry tells me, giving me a little push toward the reception desk. I find I'm eager to oblige, and I dial 911 in a flash. "Mister, I don't know what you want, but we've already told you that we have no rooms. So you might as well go," Kerry says in a far-from-friendly voice. This new, kick-ass Kerry is a Kerry I've never seen and I'm impressed. Heck, I'd go if she talked to me like that.

However, the creature is not impressed. Looking her up and down, he does what so many men have done for centuries to women — he underestimates her.

"I'm gonna get my kid," he sneers, taking a step toward her, trying to intimidate her with his fearsome five-foot-seven presence. "Are you gonna stop me?"

When he gets close enough, Kerry sighs, and quicker than you can say spit, jams several fingers into his face. In amazement, I see she has hooked his nose.

"Oh, *bon Dieu,*" he cries, falling to his knees, flapping his arms like a goose.

"Hands on your head," Kerry says conversationally. "Oh, no, no, no — don't touch your nose or I'll be forced to rip it off."

"Sshh," Kerry says. "Be quiet now. And listen." The creature listens, tears and snot running out of his nose, nodding frantically. I hear the siren of the Lavner Bay cop car turning off the highway onto our driveway but I can't take my eyes off Kerry. "We don't have your kid."

For Martha,
as always

About the Author

Lauren Wright Douglas was born in Canada in 1947. She grew up in a military family and spent part of her childhood in Europe and eastern Canada. She moved from Victoria, British Columbia, to the American southwest some years ago, but the lure of the ocean drew her westward again. Now she writes on the Oregon coast, where she lives with her partner and a variety of cats. Lauren's second novel, *Ninth Life* — a book in the Caitlin Reece series — won the Lambda Literary Award for Best Lesbian Mystery in 1990. She is presently at work on another novel.

Chapter 1

I wasn't going to be obsessive about this, but here I am, out on the porch looking for summer. I mean, the solstice or the equinox or whatever was yesterday, so where's the sun? As far as I can see the sky is the color of the stuff I dig out of my dryer's lint filter and if the aforementioned orb is anywhere up there, no one could tell. Now, I'll freely confess that I'm a tad panicky about this development because what with last December's windstorm and February's flood, sightseers have been in short supply here on the Oregon coast. A soothing piece of local wisdom has it that with Memorial Day come the tourists, much like the swallows to Capistrano, but that holiday has come and gone without producing any noticeable increase in my business. So I'm out here drinking my coffee, gnawing a hangnail, and wondering for about the hundredth time what a nice California Girl like me is doing in a place like this.

A place like this is the Oregon coast, specifically my inherited bed and breakfast in the tiny townlet of Lavner Bay — a gorgeous, quaint place of about 600 souls, inhabited by painters, potters, photographers, weavers, writers and creators of every ilk. In fact, there might be more artist-types per square foot in Lavner Bay than anyplace else on earth. I mean, when your bank manager is a photographer, the local used bookstore owner is a writer, the lady who runs Few Mornings Coffee House is a potter, and the deli gal at Spark's Market is into kelp weaving when she's not slathering sandwiches with sprouts and mayo, people like me begin to suffer from feelings of inadequacy. I don't create anything. Nor do I want to. So why am I here? Don't get me started.

In my calmer moments (i.e. the beginning of each month, when the bills are paid and unrealistic hope springs renewed in my breast) I remind myself that Lavner Bay seems a lot like Carmel before it got discovered by the talentless but moneyed art aficionados who turned it into real estate heaven and if I just wait, the same thing is bound to happen here. It's that hope which tempers my end-of-the-month resolve to sell this damned place immediately and hie myself back to the land of sun and smog. And speaking of the end of the month, it's fast approaching, bringing with it the mind-numbing prospect of Past Due notices and balancing the books (now there's an expression for you) and I feel a depression as inevitable as PMS descending upon me.

"Nuts," I say to Sam Spade, my transplanted California cat who's come to join me on the front porch. "We oughta blow this joint, Sam. I'm not cut out to be a hotelier. I'm a mail-order bookseller. Remember the fun we used to have packaging up all those hard-to-find mysteries and science fiction tomes for mailing? And you loved the ride to the post office. Remember?"

Sammy gives me one baleful yellow glare and tucks his feet underneath his body until he resembles a fat black setting hen. Poor guy, I guess he misses our erstwhile home in the brassy Mojave Desert — a dandy place if you like the color tan. Then, as if to punish me for even thinking about sun, a nasty little drizzle begins and my spirits, already low, hit bottom.

"C'mon, furball," I tell him, opening the front door. "Let's do something positive. Let's call a realtor and put this place on the market. I see a journey in our future. To someplace warm. What do you say?"

Sam joins me at the registration desk, jumping onto the counter and hoisting a leg to begin a thorough cleaning of his private parts. Taking this for a yes, I sit down, not without a twinge of guilt, to flip through my late aunt's Rolodex.

"Realtors, realtors," I'm muttering to myself when I suddenly become aware of a presence at my elbow. It's Ossie, full name Ocelot Constantine (the kid's long-fled father named the offspring after cats and the cats after parts of cars, e.g. Ocelot Constantine and her cat Overhead Cam), the B & B's blonde-haired munchkin. Daughter of Pan, our live-in handywoman, eleven-year-old Ossie has been left in my tender care while Pan attends to her ailing mother in Iowa or Utah or some such distant place, leaving me without a Jill-of-all-trades and with a responsibility I'm ill-equipped to handle. I mean, cats I understand — a little kibble, a few pats, and they're fine. But kids? The one in front of me could use a haircut, and now that I look closely, a few new clothes — her once blue T-shirt is faded and a little too short in the sleeves. BEAM ME UP, SCOTTY it says.

"Hi, Allie," Ossie says shyly. "Did you remember that we were going shopping today?" I groan because one, I didn't remember, and two, I know nothing about computers, which is what we're supposed to be going shopping for. Thanks to my late aunt's generosity, Ossie and Pan both inherited nice fat sums of money, and Pan has decided that some of it will be spent preparing Ossie for the twenty-first century. I, however, inherited an albatross — the Lavner Bay Bed & Breakfast, a business barely afloat on a sea of red ink. Gee, thanks, Aunt Grace.

The sound of a car door slamming outside distracts me from Ossie's anxious frown and I try to look businesslike, tucking the tail of my flannel shirt into my jeans and hoping I don't have peanut butter on my face.

"It's Kerry!" shrieks Ossie as a young woman in a red anorak and Dockers comes through the front door, carrying an enormous suitcase. "Will you come computer shopping with us? Do you have more luggage? Can I get it?"

"Yes, yes, and yes," Kerry Owyhee says as Ossie races out the door into the rain.

4

"Why the suitcase?" I ask. After all, Kerry lives just a mile or three down the highway and has a perfectly good bed of her own to sleep in. I can't imagine why she would want one of mine.

"The damned roof sprang another leak," she says, glowering. "It's brand new — imagine! Anyhow, after chasing the contractor up and down the coast for three days I managed to find him in Flotsam, and I think I impressed upon him the seriousness of the situation."

She glowers again and I shudder, thinking of how the conversation must have gone. Kerry can be, well, forceful. It comes from her history, I think: her Native American mother ran off from her tribe with Kerry's father who had three strikes against him — he was a non-tribe member, he worked the oil rigs, and he lured Mom away to Alaska. Anyhow, Mom went north with him, Kerry was born, Dad died in an oil-rig accident, Mom died of some godforsaken illness and the tribe in the person of Kerry's curmudgeonly aunt, refused to take Kerry back. She was fostered out and eventually adopted by a white family in Juneau, where she grew up ignorant of her roots, which is why she's back here. Looking for them. She had to develop a pretty thick skin what with being an Indian brought up by white folks, and then, when she finally located what's left of her tribe, finding less-than-welcoming relatives. She's made a little progress with Auntie, I gather, but not much. Glaciers move faster, Kerry says.

"Anyhow," she continues, tucking a wedge of gorgeous black hair behind one ear, "the contractor's promised me the work will be done in three days. So here I am. Any rooms?"

I laugh a little hysterically.

"Hmmm. Business is that bad?"

"Business is that bad."

She sighs. "Surely things will improve when summer comes."

"It is summer, toots," I tell her. "The solstice was yesterday."

"Solstice? You must be desperate if you're relying on the phases of the moon or whatever to make a difference in your business," she says archly.

I bristle. "Oh yeah? What would make a difference in my business? In your opinion."

She pulls her anorak over her head and gives me an appraising look. "Do you really want to know?"

"Kerry, I'm a phone call away from putting this place on the market. Yes, I really want to know."

"Advertising. On the Internet. Get yourself a Web page —"

I hold up a hand to stem what I fear will be a tide of technobabble. "Cool it. The only webs I have time to understand are the ones I can reach with the broom. I'm sure the Internet would be a valuable advertising medium — actually I'm not sure of that at all, but it seems like the thing to say in the latter days of the twentieth century, doesn't it? But I just don't have the time to master it. And I doubt if I have the aptitude, either. I mean, I hear about RAM and ROM and bits and bytes and my eyes glaze over."

She raises an eyebrow in eloquent skepticism. "Seriously?"

"Seriously. I had to get Ossie to load the paper into the hotel's printer. Every time I did it, it spat out origami."

She crosses her arms and looks at me in amazement. "I can see I've come just in time."

"Just in time for what?"

"Just in time to save your business. I create Web pages for companies all the time. Individuals, too. It started out as a hobby, but now it's a pretty lucrative sideline of my business. Haven't you seen my ads in *Tidal Waves*?"

"Well, no, I haven't. I've been too busy —"

"Cleaning toilets. I know." Scenting a challenge, she stands up straight, smoothing the front of her impeccably pressed tan Dockers. "Let's get started. Clearly, we haven't a moment to lose."

"I'll put the coffee on," says Ossie, handing Kerry her laptop and depositing an additional piece of luggage by the stairs. "Web pages — wow! This is too cool."

I groan, realizing that there is indeed something I loathe even more than cleaning toilets: computers. With a last wistful look at the Rolodex, I follow Ossie and Kerry into the kitchen.

Chapter 2

After about an hour of URLs, hotlinks, GIFs and other assorted bits (or were they bytes?) of cyberspeak, I figure I've had about as much of this as I can stand. Ossie and Kerry are deep into HTML or something like that, and are debating the pros and cons of JAVA. I'm ready for a java myself.

"I think I'll leave you two to the Web," I say, only half expecting an answer. They totally ignore me, as I suspected they would, so I grab my rain jacket and scoot out the back door before one of them discovers I'm not breathlessly hanging on their every word. It's not that I'm not grateful — believe me, I am — but I can take only so much of this. I mean, they may as well be speaking Swahili. Computers, to my mind, fall into the same category as cars and toilets — I want them to work when I need them, not have a deep and meaningful relationship with them, for cripe's sake.

And there's something else about computers in general and the hoopla over the Internet in particular that kinda leaves me cold: as we run to embrace the technology of the future, will we forget that the past is full of good things? Like Mr. Toad in *The Wind in the Willows,* don't we need a curmudgeonly Mr. Badger to talk us down from our manias? Mr. Badger makes some pretty good points. As Mr. Toad abandons his beloved gypsy cart for a glorious new automobile, Badger reminds us that all marvels are, after all, disposable. So there'll always be a new one. A sobering thought, because aren't we all, to some extent, Mr. Toad? And are innovations always wonderful? Consider television — isn't that a Faustian bargain if you ever saw one — a dazzling technology that induces dullness and moronism. I suspect the Internet has the same ominous tendency to bring about retrograde progress. Personally, I'd rather plunge backwards, not forward, back into books, real books, not pixels on the screen but the good, solid weight of someone's ideas and thoughts in my hands. Whenever I fear I'm becoming a Luddite about the glories of computers, I think about last winter when we were without power for almost three days. What did the technophiles do without their Internet universe of shooting stars, talking pictures, meteor showers of information? We fumbled for matches and candles and read books. They sulked. I rest my case.

Piling into my Honda Civic, I make good my escape out onto the highway and into the fog and rain.

"Crap," I grumble, noting that Few Mornings Coffee House was still in winter mode, its CLOSED sign prominently displayed. Few Mornings isn't the only game in town, as I've discovered, so I turn right at Third Street (imaginative, these Lavner Bayites) and coast to a stop in front of Frog Hollow, a weird and wonderful shop featuring crystals, tarot decks, a resident black cat, a proprietress who's a witch, and an espresso bar. I race through the rain and shake the water off my jacket in the little alcove just inside the front door. As soon as I close the door behind me, I can feel myself unwinding — a swoony piece of New Age music is playing, some lush, spicy, exotic incense is burning, and A.D. (the black cat who came after the departure of B.C.) comes to twine around my ankles. I've often thought that someone ought to write a book about coastal businesses that have cats — never have I seen such an adored assortment of worthless felines doing so little in so many establishments.

Frog Hollow's resident witch is busy doing a tarot reading for an intense-looking young man with glasses, sparse hair, and an expensive-looking red Eddie Bauer parka. Parka? In June? Definitely not a local.

A.D. leads the way into the espresso bar where *barista* Jameson and a florid, opinionated former logger are in earnest debate over the declining salmon runs, riparian erosion, and the pros and cons of fish hatcheries — all hot topics here on the coast. I order a latte and immerse myself in a table copy of *A Dictionary of Imaginary Places* — a book I had numerous requests for in the good old days when I had my own tiny business with its minuscule cares and responsibilities. I'm suddenly overcome with such a surge of longing for my small, orderly former life that it astonishes me. Were they really the good old days? I don't know, but from where I sit now, debts up the wazoo, stress that's making me a crone before my time, the past seems infinitely preferable to the present.

I swallow the rest of my latte quickly, before I begin wallowing in self-pity, and with a wave at Jameson, run out the back door and around the corner to my car. And then I realize, the miracle has happened. It's not raining. In fact, *mirabile dictu,* the sun is shining in a sky of blue the exact shade of the first VW I ever owned. I blink like an owl, looking around in amazement. Maybe it's the negative ions or something, but everything looks . . . polished. Brand new. Was there ever greener grass anywhere? Redder landscape bark? Browner dirt? And the raindrops hanging like fat crystal globes from the hydrangea leaves, what worlds might they contain?

A couple of women drive up in a snazzy red Miata with Arizona plates, and as they get out, the driver gives me a dazzling smile. I smile back then, bemused, whistling a few bars from "Hotel California," tuck a business card under one of the Miata's wipers. Climbing into my Civic, I pull out onto the highway, feeling irrationally optimistic. Maybe tourist season really is just around the corner.

11

Therefore, maybe I ought to take a peek — just a peek, mind you — at what Kerry and Ossie have cooked up. Before I throw in the towel which, I remind myself, is always an option.

Kerry and Ossie are still hard at it when I return to the B & B, and I slam the back door, hoping to break their concentration. When this fails, I decide to try English.

"Let's have a report," I say. "You guys have been into this stuff for hours."

Kerry looks up in amazement. "We have, haven't we?" Tucking her hair behind one ear, she looks at me sheepishly. "Any chance of a peanut butter sandwich? You can add it to my bill."

"Sure," I say, and Ossie springs up to do Kerry's bidding. "So what's the verdict?"

"Hmmm?" Kerry asks, her brain still idling somewhere on the information superhighway.

"This thingamajig you're going to create for me, this web or whatever, how much is it going to cost me and what do I have to do? I did hear you and Ossie utter the word *maintain* and I have to tell you that basic grooming and nutrition is about all I can maintain. I'm maxed out, Kerry. I can't take on one more responsibility. And what exactly is it going to do for me, anyhow?"

Ossie puts a sandwich in front of Kerry who takes a few thoughtful bites before answering. "Well, to answer your questions in order, nothing because you're a friend in need, nothing for the same reason I just gave, and lots, I hope. It's an advertising medium, Allison. If we link Lavner Bay Bed and

Breakfast's Web page up to, oh, even a dozen others, your occupancy rate should go through the roof."

"Really? Through the roof?"

"Sure," she says enthusiastically. "Listen, how many rooms do you have available?"

I tick them off on my fingers. "Well, we originally had six. Cordelia's gone, but I took her room, the Emilys are gone, Bree is gone, Pan and Ossie are still here . . . I think that leaves four. Yeah. Four."

"What do you charge?"

"A hundred and twenty-five a night."

"Let's see. Full occupancy would be six hundred a night. Let's aim to do that every night for the next three months."

"Okay," I say, bemused. Whatever. "But I have to tell you something."

"What?"

"I haven't the faintest idea what a Web page is or what links are or how they're going to fill my rooms. An ad I can understand. But this?"

Kerry and Ossie both look at me as if I'd just beamed down from another planet. "Oh," Kerry says. "Well, think of your Web page as an on-line brochure. With color pictures, nice blurbs about the fascinating things to do in Lavner Bay and all that. People who are browsing the Web will see it on-line —" She pauses here. "You do know what on-line is, don't you?"

I nod uncertainly. "Yeah." Then I wonder. Do I? "No," I reply, which elicits more horrified looks from the cybernaughts.

"Oh," says Ossie.

"Brother," Kerry replies.

"Is the Web the Net?" I ask. "Like in the movie with Sandra Bullock?"

"Yes and no," Kerry says. "It's, well, it's ... the Net isn't really anything. There are, gosh, I don't know, maybe thirty million computers all over the world, all potentially linked together with, um, with software."

"So the Web and the Net *are* the same thing?"

Kerry chews her lip. "Let's say they are. It'll make things easier to understand."

I am more than a little nonplused. I mean, if the cyberspeakers didn't really understand this Web and Net business, how could a Badger like me be expected to fathom it? "Okay," I say patiently. "So there are these zillions of computers linked together with software. How does that help me?"

"Just think for a minute," Kerry says enthusiastically. "Someone in, say, Portland or Vancouver or New York City is surfing the Net, browsing Oregon coast vacation spots one dreary winter night. And they come across Lavner Bay Bed & Breakfast. Your establishment knocks their socks off with its fabulous photos, great graphics and clever prose. So they e-mail you and make a reservation."

Ossie giggles. I stare. "Really?" I say.

"Really."

"How, um, how will you get the photos? And the prose?"

"I have a photographer friend who owes me a favor. No problem. And I can take some myself."

"And the clever prose?"

"I'll get some brochures from the Chamber of Commerce and give them a makeover. You'll need to supply some facts about the B & B. And Ossie wants to contribute some bits of local history she's been collecting."

I look at the munchkin in amazement. "You have?"

She looks down modestly at the tabletop. "We had to do a school project," she says. "I got an A."

I look at the two of them — such eagerness, such optimism. Why didn't I share it? Maybe I've cleaned one too many toilets. "Well, what are you waiting for?" I ask them, feigning an enthusiasm I don't quite feel. "Apparently, I have nothing to lose, and if you two want to spend some time on this little project, go to it."

Ossie shrieks in delight. "Yes!"

"Go get your jacket," Kerry tells her. "We'll pick up your computer when we get the things I need." She's off up the stairs like a shot.

"This is awfully, well, nice of you," I tell Kerry. "Are you sure you have the time for it?"

She shrugs. "I'm out of my house for a few days. Might as well do something productive. And it'll be good practice."

"Hey, will this really not cost me anything?"

"I'll look for some free spots first," she says. "When this starts costing you money, I'll let you know."

I sit back and look at her, a tiny suspicion

growing in my mind. No one with a successful business has this much free time. "So, um, how's business for you?" I ask.

She laughs a little. "Let's just say that Coast Investigations isn't making me rich."

"I'm sorry to hear that," I tell her. "I know how much you wanted an investigations business of your own."

She shrugs. "Yeah. But I guess that was an unrealistic ambition. On the other hand, I may be able to turn my computer hobby into a business. I'm not complaining. It seems that a lot more people want to learn about technology than want to learn who's stealing money from their company or who their husband's seeing in his off hours."

I laugh. "Maybe that's a good thing, you know, looking toward the future instead of dwelling on the past."

She gives me a searching look and in response, I grin sheepishly. "Hmm. Do I detect just a little hint of depression?" she asks.

I shake my head. "More than a little, Kerry. If business doesn't pick up, I'll have to sell this place. I know it isn't what Aunt Grace would have wanted, but even I am enough of a businesswoman to recognize red ink. Hell, I'm drowning in it."

"I'm ready!" Ossie announces from the hall.

Kerry walks me to the registration desk where Sam Spade has made himself comfortable in the middle of everything. "About Ossie's computer."

"Oh yeah. Pan said she could spend fifteen hundred dollars." I take an envelope out of a locked drawer and hand it to Kerry.

"Your Aunt Grace was a pretty generous woman,"

Kerry says, stuffing the envelope into the back pocket of her Dockers. "I mean, maybe you need to take into consideration the fact that she built this place for reasons other than to make money."

"I know that," I tell her patiently, "but we can't keep going without making some money. I mean, there's a difference between breaking even and going under."

"Let's hold a good thought," Kerry says. "Maybe you won't have to sell. Maybe technology will make a difference."

"That'll be the day," I mutter ungraciously, but my mumblings fall on absent ears.

Chapter 3

I'm sitting at the registration desk with Sammy, trying to get caught up with some paperwork, when who comes through the front door but the pair from Frog Hollow. The women with the Miata. Heck, maybe I should slip business cards under more windshield wipers.

"Oh, hi," the taller of the two says, recognizing me. She is, I note, the one who gave me the dazzling smile, and she now repeats it. Wow. Curly brown hair, blue eyes, a tan that doesn't quite hide freckles, a pale blue denim shirt tucked into jeans, and a pair of Nike hiking boots — this is an outdoorsy lass for sure. Her companion is slightly older, femmier, longer- haired, thinner, and less overtly friendly than the smiler, but her long-sleeved black T-shirt that says 1995 Victoria Marathon tells me that she's no slouch in the athletic department, either. "Hi," the smiler says again. "Do you have any rooms?"

I try not to giggle. Do we have any rooms? "As a matter of fact, you're in luck," I tell her, lying shamelessly. "We've had a cancellation, so we have quite a nice room available. It's a hundred and twenty-five dollars a night."

She gives me a conspiratorial smile. "Katherine, we're in luck," she calls to her companion. The aforementioned Katherine drifts over, bestows a possessive look on her partner, smiles, says, "How nice," then drifts away again to study the map of hiking trails I've affixed to one wall of the lobby.

Sensing a little discord between the two, I look to the smiler for guidance. "How, um, many nights would you like to stay?"

The smile fades a little. "Three or four. I'm not exactly sure. Can I tell you later?" She hands over her VISA card and I run it through the machine, giving her one of our registration cards to fill out. She completes it, hands it back and I note that her name is Eve. Be still my heart. "You can have Number Four," I tell her. "It's on the second floor. It has a great view of the ocean." Then I go into my spiel. "We serve a continental breakfast starting at eight every morning in the parlor on the second floor — juice, a fruit salad, muffins, bagels, coffee, tea, hot chocolate. There's a coffee maker and a hot plate there so you can have hot drinks anytime you want.

A microwave, too. You might want to make popcorn. There's a big-screen TV in the parlor and a VCR. We have a nice selection of movies on tape." I can see I'm losing her because her glance keeps straying to Cool Kathy, so I wind up my presentation. "There's only one phone — it's over there on the coffee table. I'd appreciate it if you use a calling card to make long-distance calls. We have a fax machine if you need to send or receive anything. There are menus for local restaurants on the coffee table and I'd be happy to answer any questions you might have about things to do."

Katherine gives Eve a come-hither look and Eve flashes one last apologetic smile in my direction. I hand her the key and she follows Katherine up the stairs. For heaven's sake, aren't they even going to go get their luggage? As Kerry would say, brother. Then I realize they're probably just taking a look at the room, not ripping each other's clothes off and falling on the bed in wild abandon. I tidy up the registration desk, filing Eve's card and VISA slip, and Sam Spade returns from a brief feline walkabout.

"You missed them, " I tell him. "The first guests of the summer and you weren't here to play host." He looks at me doubtfully. "No, Kerry doesn't count. So what do you think? Is this a sign of things to come — guests flocking in like seagulls at low tide?" He yawns, indifferent to the imperatives of business. After all, his kibble bowl gets filled no matter what. Half an hour later, when the gals in Number Four still haven't made an appearance, I realize that yes, they probably are upstairs writhing in the throes of passion, so I take myself and my cat out onto the back deck to sit in the sun and try not to be envious. I mean, it's been so long since I writhed with anyone that maybe I've forgotten how. I've just started thinking about this potentially depressing situation when who comes around the corner of the house but Eve, looking self-conscious and smiling a very small smile indeed. Various greetings spring to mind, and I censor half a dozen before a sufficiently innocuous one presents itself. "Getting settled in?" I ask.

She nods, looking out over the ocean which has turned cobalt blue under the mid-afternoon sun. "What a gorgeous place," she says. "It's always been a dream of mine to own a bed and breakfast on the ocean. How did you swing it?"

I bite back a laugh, amazed that so many people I run into want to give up their perfectly nice jobs and come to the coast to clean toilets and fret. "How did I swing it? I didn't. The B & B was left to me by my aunt. She died last year."

"Don't you just love it?" she enthuses.

"Not so far," I tell her truthfully. "I mean, I love this place, but no, I don't love running the B & B."

"Oh," she says, clearly disappointed in me.

"I'm not a people person," I explain. "Running this place has been good for me in that I've come to realize that fact about myself. I suspected it before, but now, alas, I know it's true," I say, trying to make light of the subject. "I'd be better off with inanimate objects. Books, maybe," I say wistfully, realizing as I utter these words how much I really do miss my old business. I used to get strange and wonderful missives from my book-seekers — some of them written on napkins from McDonald's, some of them written on gorgeous, exotic postcards or note-

21

cards. And some of them weren't written at all. I had one client who just sent me reviews ripped from magazines or newspapers. I would then take the requested title and go to work calling around to my sources — rare and used books dealers all across the country. Someone somewhere always had the book my client wanted. And because I restricted myself to fields I was familiar with — mysteries and science fiction/fantasy — I always knew if the price was fair. I added a percentage for myself, called the client back, and *voilà* — a sale. And I never even had to get out of my T-shirt and shorts to do business. Suddenly I realize that Eve is looking at me oddly. I clear my throat, recalling myself to the present. "But here I am," I say.

"Here you are," she confirms.

"What about you?" I ask. "Are you a people person?" Ha. I should have asked her about her tolerance for toilet-cleaning.

"Definitely," she says, showing me her perfectly capped teeth again in a huge smile, and I groan, my attraction to her fading. It's suddenly hit me that Eve is one of those people who beam indiscriminately. No wonder Cool Kate is a trifle short with her from time to time. Still, indiscriminate beaming would be a good quality in a hotelier.

"Ah, there you are," says a frosty voice from behind us.

"Katherine!" Eve exclaims, beaming on her too. "Our hostess was just telling me what it takes to run a bed and breakfast."

I hold out my hand to Katherine. "Allison O'Neil," I offer. "Late of Lancaster, California, now resident of the soggiest town in America."

Katherine tries hard not to laugh and loses the struggle. "Katherine Prentiss," she says, shaking my hand. "Owning a bed and breakfast is one of Eve's dreams. Of course, so is climbing Everest and sailing the Pacific single-handed." She bestows on Eve a patronizing smirk and I decide these ladies deserve each other. I'm done trying to be friendly.

"Well, enjoy yourselves, folks," I tell them, getting up and brushing off my jeans. "A hotelier never rests. I'm off to do some paperwork." I leave them on the deck in contemplation of the ocean, or each other, and beat a hasty retreat into the kitchen. There I take several cookbooks off the shelf and sit down for a guilty perusal of cookie recipes. I have a confession: I derive the same pleasure from furtively paging through cookbooks that other people seem to derive from erotica — spoonfuls of silky butter, cool and slippery on the lips; the slow, delicious stickiness of honey; the mysterious, musky darkness of chocolate . . . I sit back and close my eyes, imagining the separate delights of cookie ingredients. Then, with a shiver, I slam the book closed and try to compose myself. And none too soon either. The bell on the inside of the front door tinkles. I hastily shelve the well-worn cookbook and poke my head around the kitchen door. It's Kerry, looking worried.

"Well?" I ask. "Where's the loot? Ossie's computer and printer and so on." I look around, puzzled. "Where's Ossie?"

"In the car," Kerry says in a strange voice.

I'm alarmed now. "Kerry, you're scaring me. Is something wrong with Ossie?"

She shakes her head. "Ossie's okay. It's not that. It's just that we . . . well, Ossie —"

"I'll tell her," Ossie says, closing the door quietly behind her. I look at her closely.

"Where's your jacket?" I ask, parental.

"Minou's wearing it," she says, looking guilty.

"Of course she is," I say, finally getting it. Ossie's found another of a seemingly endless series of stray cats and has brought it home, wrapped in her jacket. "Well, go get it."

She gives me an incredulous look.

"Go on. It's probably hungry. We'll give it a bowl of milk. No big deal."

She hesitates.

"Go on," Kerry says. "We'll figure this out."

"What's the problem?" I ask as Ossie scoots out the door. "What's she found? A mom and litter? Or something bigger? A cougar?"

"Um," Kerry says, and now I'm *really* worried.

"What, Kerry? Oh, hell, it's not a wild thing is it? Because she knows we can't keep wild animals." I suddenly remember an event from last spring. "If it's another baby seal, I'll strangle her."

"No it's not a seal," Ossie says, pushing something through the door. Something reluctant. Something small. Something that looks an awful lot like a kid. It swipes a tangled mane of dark hair off its face with a grimy paw and I see that it is indeed a kid — the filthiest one I've ever laid eyes on.

"This is Minou," Ossie says. "She was living in a refrigerator box behind Safeway. She's all alone. We have to help her."

Chapter 4

Ossie's upstairs supervising Minou's bath and I'm in the kitchen giving Kerry hell.

"Ossie I can understand, but you? You're an adult, a grown person, with a grown person's brain. You know we can't let her stay here."

"Why not?" Kerry asks, belligerent, arms folded across her chest. "She has to stay somewhere."

"Why not? I'll tell you why not! Because . . . because . . . dammit, because this isn't a halfway house for the indigent!"

Kerry raises an eyebrow. "No?"

And then I remember what my aunt intended when she built the bed and breakfast — that it serve also as a safe place, a haven. So if I'm going to run it as she ran it, I have no right to turn Minou away, now do I? I sit down heavily at the table, overcome.

"This is how it starts, isn't it?" I ask Kerry.

"What do you mean?"

"You know perfectly well what I mean — this is how one starts acquiring loonies. Remember when I took over the B & B? Remember the nut cases we had living here — the Emilys, Cordelia the Grey, the cat writer? They may have been down and out at one time, but Grace just let them . . . stay. Gratis. And — "

Kerry holds up a hand, interrupting my panicky babbling. "Whoa, girl. No one's asking you to let the kid stay forever. But surely you'll agree that we couldn't leave her living in a box behind Safeway?"

"What were you doing behind Safeway, anyhow?" I ask to avoid answering the question.

"Oh, you know Ossie. She thought she saw a cat with a limp run around the corner. She did — it was Minou's cat. Or at least a cat that lived in the box with her."

I shake my head. Ossie and her strays. "Okay so you couldn't leave the kid there. What about Child Protective Services?"

"It's Saturday," she reminds me.

I grind my teeth. "What about the cops? Couldn't they, well, take care of her?"

She shrugs. "We could call them, and they might come out and take her — if they had time. But because she's in no danger they'd give our call a pretty low priority. And they'd just hand her over to

CPS on Monday anyhow. So she might as well stay here until then."

"Stay here?" I yell. "Wait a minute. For crap's sake, doesn't she have *anyone*? Where's her mother?"

"In the county jail."

"Oh. Well, how about the father?"

"She doesn't know. Or won't say. She's pretty evasive about him. I suspect he's who she was running away from."

"Nice. Relatives?"

"An aunt. In Louisiana."

"Louisiana? As in the state?"

"Yeah."

"Jeez." I rake one hand through my hair, reminding myself that no, she's not going to be here forever. Or even as long as the Emilys or that dippy cat writer. "Okay, here's what we'll do. She can have a bath, a square meal, and a good night's sleep —"

Kerry gives me a glower.

"Okay, maybe two. But come Monday morning we do it by the book. She goes to CPS. Agreed?"

She looks so solemn at this that I drum my fingers on the table, wondering why Kerry's being so . . . unreasonable. And then I remember that *she* was packed off to CPS after her mother's death. Yikes. Of course Kerry will have some pretty bad memories. Still, the kid can't stay here. I'm not budging on that.

"Okay?" I repeat, and she nods. "We'll clean her up, let her get a good night's sleep or two, give her some clean clothes and then . . ." I wait for Kerry to acknowledge that yes, the kid has to be placed in the care of the proper authorities, but she changes the subject.

"Whatever. Anyhow, if that's it about Minou, I'll go get Ossie's stuff out of the car and start setting it up. She'll be dying to use her computer."

"Whatever," I echo, not really listening, and Kerry sets off for the car. At this point, I'm happy to be left alone because I'm disturbed, really disturbed. Not so much about the kid — I can get rid of her come Monday — but about the fact that Kerry seems to be identifying with her, for cripe's sake! I mean, the CPS folks aren't ogres.

And I'm disturbed, too, about my responsibilities to Aunt Grace. Or rather to the spirit of Aunt Grace — specifically to her wishes — which I've never really analyzed because, I guess, I'm reluctant to come to grips with them. What am I expected to be, anyhow — the Mother Teresa of the Oregon Coast? I'm too young for that kind of philanthropy. And a kid? I'd have to apply to CPS to be a foster parent, a horrible prospect if ever there was one. I put my head in my hands and close my eyes, willing all this away. But of course it won't go.

I need to talk to someone, I decide. One of Aunt Grace's cronies, one of the friends who knew her best. I grab my jacket, and meet Kerry on the stairs.

"Will you watch the place for me for a couple of hours?"

She looks at me suspiciously. "Okay. Are you all right?"

"Yes. No." I shrug. "Who knows? I need to talk to someone about —" I make an all-encompassing gesture. "About all this. I don't know if I can run this place the way Grace would have wanted me to. I don't think I have that kind of compassion." Nor do I have the slightest interest in kids, I add mentally, shuddering.

Kerry looks doubtful. "Evidently she thought you did or she wouldn't have left the place to you."

I feel suddenly trapped. "Yeah, but now that I'm being put to the test, I feel angry and resentful. This is a business. I mean, I want that kid gone. Out of here. I don't want another responsibility. I'm up to here with responsibilities, Ker."

Kerry frowns, clearly concerned. "Hey, if I came on too strong about the kid —"

I shake my head.

"Sure," she says. "I'll watch the desk for a while. Who are you going to talk to?"

"Someone whose business it is to listen."

I find my spirits improving the farther I drive from the B & B and this makes me feel guilty all over again. There's something about driving that makes me feel optimistic, as though the road ahead might lead to unguessed possibilties, and for one giddy instant I'm tempted to keep on going, to put the hammer down, the pedal to the metal, and roar though Windsock, Sea Lion Rock, and Drizzle Bay, up to Landlubber City and Seattle or maybe the moon. Do it, a little voice urges. Put all this behind you. Blow it all off. Alarmed at how intently I'm listening to this siren song, I pull off the road at one of the little state parks and find a spot overlooking the ocean. You cannot run away, I tell myself sternly. You owe it to Aunt Grace. Yeah, well, that's just the problem, isn't it? What do I owe Aunt Grace? It's not as if she left me the B & B with strings attached or anything. I mean, there was no sealed letter making her wishes plain. I had to . . . infer them, deduce them, for cripe's sake. Just because she felt moved to give sanctuary to seemingly every down-on-her-luck loony who drove down Highway 101, do I have to do the same? And now the universe is sending runaway kids to the B & B!

As I'm reminded every month when I pay the bills, Grace had enough money that she could afford to subsidize her philanthropic inclinations. But I don't. The B & B is slowly, inexorably going under. I look out at the ocean and the sight, which usually soothes me and makes me think metaphysical thoughts, just agitates me. I mean, anyone in her right mind would give a leg or some other significant body part to be sitting here, right here, where I am, contemplating a truly astonishing expanse of sand cluttered only by seagulls and driftwood, an ocean as blue as a Wedgewood plate, and a sky the exact hue of a powder blue poodle skirt I saw in a vintage clothing shop in Portland last winter. All this and not a soul around, except for one of the ever-hopeful and ravenous coast ravens (someone told me they're really crows, but I prefer to think of them as ravens). I mean, the beach is utterly *empty*. What a place to contemplate nature, or the meaning of life, or to recite all the verses of "The Walrus and the Carpenter," or even "Dover Beach." Oh God, not

"Dover Beach." I must be in a funk. Maybe like the raven, I need to eat. Maybe my blood sugar is low. Maybe I need to switch to decaf. Maybe I need a new life.

Sighing, I get back into my Civic and pull out into traffic, slowing as I enter downtown (ha — all twenty-seven shopfronts of it) Windsock. A smidgen bigger than Lavner Bay, it has many of the modern conveniences that LB lacks, boasting, among other things, one bookstore, two gas stations, three churches, four banks, five motels, six espresso establishments, seven coffee shops (but alas, no really nice restaurant), eight real estate offices and, for all I know, nine drummers drumming. I pass a sign on a realty office that always cracks me up. FREE ADVICE, it proclaims. I wonder if I should stop in. Nah. I'll get something to eat. Works better than therapy any time.

The Daily Grind is doing a land-office business what with this being a sunny summer Saturday, so there's nary a seat to be had on the deck. I take my cheese-stuffed baked potato and my bottle of Snapple and go sit at the picnic table on the lawn, planning to eat and brood, but Kaye, the perky blonde proprietress of the Grind, comes out of the kitchen to sit with me.

"You're busy," I say enviously.

"Summer," she tells me matter-of-factly. "We'll all be busy soon. You'll see."

"Ha. It may be too late for me."

"You're not thinking what I think you're thinking, are you?"

"If you mean am I thinking of selling, the answer's yes. I'm thinking about it."

This clearly surprises her but now that I've said the words, they seem right. I've been aware that my subconscious has been playing solitaire with this idea for some months, but sometimes you have to say things out loud to make them real.

"Sorry to hear that," Kaye says.

"Don't be," I tell her. "I know that my aunt hoped I'd, you know, follow in her footsteps, but I don't think I'm meant to be a hotelier."

"Will you stay around here or go back to California?"

"I'd like to stay here. Either in Windsock or Lavner Bay." And now that I've uttered these words, they seem right, too.

She snaps her fingers. "Say, I've just remembered — there were a couple of women in here yesterday. One of them was inquiring about whether I knew of any coastal businesses for sale."

"Oh yeah?" I answer, only half-interested. I mean, every other woman who passes through a coastal town develops an urge to open a business there, doesn't she? It must be in the water.

Someone yells for her from the kitchen and she smiles, patting my arm. "Gotta go. Things will work out. Don't worry."

As I finish my Snapple, I wonder if I oughtn't to be going to see a realtor instead of the place I'm headed, but what the heck, I'm almost there. And a little baring of the soul couldn't hurt. I need to talk to someone about Aunt Grace and what she intended and the fact that I don't think I'm made of the stuff she thought I was and, most of all, what in hell can I do about it and still look at myself in the mirror in the mornings.

Chapter 5

The Metamorphosis Center is just as I remember it from last summer — a cheery yellow bungalow down by the dock. It has a terrific view of the Chelsea River, which leads to the bay of the same name, and today the water is a deep, dark, mysterious slate gray against the wooded hill on the opposite bank. As I find a place in the public parking lot next to the crab ring rental hut, I see one of the bay's seals surface, its speckled head silently breaking the water. It hears me close the car door and turns, fixing me with huge brown eyes.

"Good fishing today?" I ask it and it blinks lazily, completely unconcerned by my presence. I've come to love these critters in particular, and it always gives me a visceral kind of thrill to see them pop their sleek heads above the water and look around with those wonderful brown eyes. In my more fanciful moments, I wonder if they aren't messengers from earth's other kingdom — the watery one, the one that comprises most of our planet — and if we pay very close attention, couldn't we understand what they seem to want to tell us? I know that's silly, but I always take some extra time when I see a seal. Just in case.

The gate in the Metamorphosis Center's white picket fence has a new latch — in fact, the paint job looks fresh too, and I can detect signs of just-planted flowers in the neat beds. All this industry. I think of the sorry state the B & B's flower beds are in now that the Emilys have departed and wonder, not for the first time, who's going to take care of them. Pan is great with protesting motors, balky doors, frizzled wiring, broken pipes, and other mechanical problems, but foliage isn't her long suit. Nor mine. I've never had a garden. Well, I had an indoor herb garden once but when I wasn't overwatering it, Sammy was nibbling it to death. I haven't the faintest idea how to proceed. Anyhow, I'm lost in admiration of a particularly gorgeous bed of purple, mauve, and lavender pansies, just vegging out with the sun on my back, and the smell of growing things and freshly dug earth in my nose, so I don't hear someone come up behind me until they speak.

"Allison," a pleasant voice says. "I saw you get out of your car. I hoped you were coming here."

I turn. It's Robin, the Center's owner, with a flat of dark blue lobelia in her hands. A trim, middle-aged woman with salt-and-pepper hair, sunburned nose, oversized blue-checked work shirt, and grass-stained jeans, Robin was one of my aunt's dearest friends. "These can wait a bit," she tells me. "C'mon inside." She puts the flat down in the shade of a huckleberry bush, brushes her hands on her jeans and takes my arm. "I haven't seen you all winter," she chides. "Where have you been hiding?"

"Oh, you know," I mumble. "At the B & B. There always seems to be something to do."

"There always will be," she says, leading me into the kitchen. "Grace used to say that no matter how much or how little you do, there's always something else." I take a seat at her cheery blue table, on a red chair with a yellow poppy painted on its seat, and wait while she fills the kettle and rummages around in the cupboard for mugs. It's so quiet and darn it, peaceful in here. I can hear birds cheeping faintly through an open window over the sink and as I turn to listen, the lace curtains flutter in a breeze. A warm breeze. Suddenly I realize that yes, it really is summer. I sigh. It seems as though I've spent the whole winter with my head in one toilet or another, worrying about money. Dammit, I don't want to spend the summer that way, and certainly not the rest of my life.

My distress must have registered on my face. "As much as I'd like to think this is a social call, it isn't, is it?" Robin says, putting a mug of fragrant tea in front of me.

"No," I mumble, feeling guilty because I really had intended to come and see Robin, to get to know

36

her, but there always seemed to be something — some awkwardness, a reluctance to talk about Aunt Grace, something I couldn't quite name — holding me back. "I'm a soul who needs a metamorphosis," I say, only half joking.

"Tell me about it," she says, blowing on her tea, blue eyes earnest.

A tentative touch on my knee breaks my concentration and I look down to see Amberilla, Robin's fluffy orange cat. "Me now?" she asks, plainly wanting to be picked up. I'm happy to oblige her.

"It's the B & B," I tell Robin. "I know it meant a great deal to Grace, but I don't think I'm the right person to run it."

"Grace must have thought you were," she says, echoing Kerry's sentiments. "Otherwise she wouldn't have left it to you."

This makes me irritable, but I try to keep the testiness out of my voice. "Well, the thing is that I hadn't even talked to Grace for a number of years and I think that in the intervening time I became someone different from the person she remembered. Is this making sense?" She nods, encouraging me, and I plunge on. "When I was younger, before my mother died, I think I was a nicer person. More generous. Oh, I don't know — I was trying to be what Mom and Aunt Grace wanted me to be. Was that generous or was that just spineless? I was an only child. They doted on me. I never even thought about what I might want."

"And now?"

"Well — and I don't think this is necessarily a bad thing — I've become selfish, you know? Now I'm interested in finding out what I really want instead of trying to please other people." I laugh. "It's a whole lot easier now because there's no one left to try to please."

"Sure there is," Robin says. "There's Grace."

Irritation prickles in me again and I almost blurt out, *No there isn't, Grace is dead, dammit.* But I don't. "That's why I'm so upset. It sounds ungrateful, doesn't it, to be resentful of this wonderful gift, this B & B, this ready-made business. But it's got some pretty big strings attached to it." I'm quiet for a minute, wondering how much to tell Robin. Then I figure what the hell and just go for it. "When my mother died, I kind of went into shock for a while, but eventually I made a job, a business for myself. I loved what I was doing."

"What were you doing?" Robin asks, plainly curious.

"Well," I reply diffidently, suddenly self-conscious about my enthusiasm, "it might not be everyone's idea of a thrilling business, but I had — well, I still have it but I hardly work at it anymore — a mail-order book business. I specialize in hard-to-find mysteries and science fiction/fantasy. I pretty much know the serious collectors. The book dealers, too. See, somebody might ask me to find, say, a first edition of *The Moon Pool,* and I'd get on the phone and make some calls. If I couldn't find it right away, I might have to go scout around to second-hand bookstores."

Robin smiles. "You should have seen your face as you talked about finding books. You just . . . glowed. Books. They're your real love, aren't they?"

Traitor that I am, I tell her the truth. "Yes."

"And the B & B?"

"I feel trapped there," I say. "Let me give you an

example. Today my handywoman's daughter brought home this, this . . . waif. A kid she found living in a box behind Safeway. Ragged, dirty, smelly. God knows what she's been through. I suppose I should have been more compassionate. Grace would have been. But instead of being generous and caring, I freaked. I totally lost it."

"Sounds as though you were frightened," she says.

Frightened? I hadn't thought about that. I figured I was just feeling penny-pinching, put-upon, parsimonious. In a word, resentful. Resentful that I would have to spend my time and energy and the B & B's few resources on yet another problem. But now that I think about it, I realize that yeah, maybe I was frightened. I consider this for a moment. "You know, maybe what frightened me was that I saw this kid not as herself, an individual, but as, what, a symbol? A symbol of what's expected of me."

"And what do you think is expected of you?"

I take a deep breath. "That I take in the lame, halt, and blind of the world." I see Robin wince and I'm suddenly annoyed. "Well? I don't know. Isn't that what Grace did?"

"Did she?"

"Robin, I'm totally over my head with all this. I mean, who did she decide to let stay for nothing and who did she turn away? How did she choose?"

"Did you ever consider that maybe she didn't."

This kind of mumbo-jumbo upsets me so much that I dump Amberilla unceremoniously onto the floor. "That she didn't? What do you mean?"

"Maybe they — the people who needed help — maybe they chose. Think about it. How many people have you had knocking on the door asking for help?"

"Well, none. Until the kid."

She gives me an eloquent look.

"Okay, okay," I concede. "So maybe there won't be hordes of indigents descending on the B & B. But even one is too many for me. I mean, Aunt Grace had resources of her own. I don't. Therefore, every time a deadbeat —" there's that wince again, but I'm fired up, so I just forge on — "takes up one of my rooms, I'm out a hundred and a quarter a night." I run a hand through my hair, really agitated now. "I mean, here's my friend Kerry trying to bail out my sinking business by getting me on the Web or the Net or whatever and here I am giving rooms away because a wealthy philanthropist thought it was a neat thing to do. Doesn't that seem a little, well, illogical?"

"Yes," Robin says, "I can see how you might have a problem with it."

"Thanks," I say, sitting back, a little surprised that she's not disagreeing with me. But I don't feel that she's totally on my side, either. Well, dammit, what did I expect? She was Grace's friend, not mine.

"So," she says, sipping her tea, "what do you propose to do about the situation?"

Amberilla has vaulted into my lap again, sensing my dismay, and I hug her a little too hard, making her wriggle. "Hell, I don't know. Something, though." I finish my tea and put the mug down on the table.

"As I see it, you have two problems," Robin says. "One, you're not doing what you really love doing. Your book business."

I nod, amazed that I had to hear someone else say it to make it real. "And two?"

"Two, that you're being forced to do what someone else loved doing."

I smile bitterly because that's the truth in a nutshell. Oh, Aunt Grace, what have you done?

"So now that you've identified the problems, what are you going to do about them?" she asks.

I bury my face in Amberilla's fur. "I don't know. Something, though. I sure have to do something." I put Amberilla gently down on the floor and look at my watch. "It'll soon be supper time. I'd better let you get back to your flowers."

She walks me to the front gate and holds it open for me. "I know you're distressed, but try not to worry too much about this, okay?"

I resist the urge to laugh. Sure. I won't worry a bit. Robin must see the manic glint in my eyes because she lays a hand on my arm.

"I mean it, Allison. People choose to live here on the coast because they want simpler lives, not more complicated ones. If you see the B & B and everything that ownership of it implies as an unwelcome chore, as a crazy-maker, then it will be." She cocks her head and looks at me. "I believe you already know what you have to do."

Feeling like a worm, I look away guiltily because yeah, I guess I do know.

Chapter 6

Back at the B & B things are, according to Kerry who is personing the registration desk, coming along swimmingly.

"Everything's under control," she reassures me, looking crisp and professional in her oatmeal fisherman-knit sweater and unwrinkled tan pants. She's put one of my Windham Hill CDs on the sound system and the lobby feels peaceful. "We have another pair of guests," she informs me with off-handed pride. "I put them in Number Two."

I'm amazed. I go away for an hour and look what

happens. "Fabulous," I tell her. "How long are they going to stay?"

"All week." She grins, pleased with herself.

"Better and better. Maybe I can pay the electric bill after all. So, where's Ossie."

"In the kitchen. I'm letting her use my computer — hers doesn't have the programs we need to get the B & B launched on the information superhighway. She's typing her local history stuff into a file. I'll edit it and then we'll load it into the Web page I've designed for you."

Ah that. How can I tell Kerry the traitorous thoughts that have been zooming around in my mind. Well, there'll be time enough for all that. Besides, I'm sure that the B & B's new owner will be thrilled to be online. There, I've thought it: the B & B's new owner. Amazed at myself, I stop dead in my tracks.

"Something wrong?" Kerry asks.

"No, something's right," I reply, elated. I've actually acknowledged possibilities. My own power. Maybe there really can be Life After B & B Ownership. Maybe the ghost of Aunt Grace wouldn't haunt me after all if I sold this place. With a lighter step, I whistle a few bars of "On the Road Again" and go on into the kitchen to see what Ossie's up to.

As I suspected, what Ossie's up to is pretty much incomprehensible, so I content myself with reading the bits of local history she's extracted from her school project. After all, it wouldn't hurt to know what's going into or onto my own Web page, now would it?

"Where in heck is Swimming Cat Cove?" I ask her, picking up an astonishingly well-written page titled "Coastal Oddities." As well as Swimming Cat

Cove, the page contains a discussion of Preacher's Cave, Ghost Rocks, and The Maelstrom. Deliciously creepy stuff.

"Just down the coast three or four miles," she says. "It's my favorite of all the coast stories."

"Hmmm," I say, reading this tale of wonder. It seems that a fishing boat named the Amanda Lee went aground on the rocks at the entrance to the cove during a terrible storm about 70 years ago. All hands were lost except for the ship's cat, which managed to swim to shore and scale the nearly unscalable cliffs. Rescuers who attempted to reach the Amanda Lee found the cat — who looked astonishingly fit and dry — on the bluffs above the cove the next day, and the spot has been called Swimming Cat Cove ever since.

"Wait a minute," I say in healthy skepticism. "How did the rescuers know it was the ship's cat? It could have been a neighborhood stray."

Ossie gives me a look of withering scorn. "The cat's collar had a tag on it that said Amanda Lee. It's all in paragraph two."

Chastened, I read on to paragraph two where Ossie related the story of the cat's collar and speculated that the cat could have found a small cave or crevice in the rocks where it kept dry until morning, whereupon it scaled the cliff and waited for rescue. Ossie concluded the story with a caveat for explorers: "Swimming Cat Cove is only passable at low tide," she warned, "because the water comes halfway up the cliffs when the tide is in. And it is no place for children at any time."

"Do they pay attention?" I ask Ossie.

"Who?"

"Children. Do they stay away from the cove?"

She looks thoughtful. "Mostly. It's a pretty dangerous place. A couple of boys from the high school got stuck just above the high tide line last year. The Coast Guard had to rescue them. They didn't say anything, but everyone knew they were pretty scared."

I'm impressed. No wonder the kid got an A.

"Well?" Ossie asks, looking up shyly from her typing. Do you want it on your Web page?"

"Sure. It's great local color."

She clicks away for a few more minutes while I watch her, amazed at her talent.

"You're a good writer," I tell her and she ducks her head.

"Oh, I don't know," she says off-handedly.

"Of course you are," I repeat. "Your teachers must tell you that. Don't you believe them?"

She stops typing and looks up at me, gray eyes troubled. "Yeah, I believe them. But Mom says writing won't put potatoes on the table."

I bristle at this. On the one hand I want to encourage an 11-year-old's talent, but on the other, I don't want to dismiss Pan's concern. "It's true that most poets or novelists can't make a living at what they do," I tell her. "But there are plenty of other ways to use your writing to put potatoes on the table."

"Yeah?" she says hopefully.

"Sure. When you're older, you could write for a newspaper. Or a magazine. Or write —" I gesture at the pages on the table, "stuff like that. Ossie, I bet you could put these stories — and a couple more — into little booklets and sell them to motel and B & B owners. Tourists would love it."

"Yeah?" she asks, clearly amazed.

"Yeah."

She looks off into space, bemused. Then, out of left field, she says, "I have to tell you something about Minou."

"Who? Oh, yeah. Minou."

"Well, it's about her father, really. You see, the reason she was living in that box behind Safeway is that she's, um, afraid of him."

My heart soars — so there *is* another family member lurking around somewhere! Maybe we won't have to wait until Monday. And as for being afraid, well for cripe's sake, maybe it's just the usual kids-versus-dads stuff. Maybe he wouldn't let her watch cartoons or MTV or whatever it is that normal kids watch too much of. (Ossie, I remind myself is not normal. All she watches is *Star Trek* in all its incarnations, *The X-Files*, *The Outer Limits,* and nature programs with the sound turned off. She says she doesn't want to learn anything sad about the animals.) Or maybe Minou didn't clean up her room or do her chores. A father! I can hardly wait. "Did she tell you where they were living?" I ask. "We really ought to call him. He's probably worried sick."

Ossie looks at me as though a purple horn has sprouted from the middle of my forehead. "Minou's afraid of him," she repeats. "She doesn't want to go back there."

"Go back where?" Kerry says from behind me.

Ossie gets up and hurries over to Kerry, who puts a protective arm around the kid's shoulders. I groan, seeing an alliance forming. "We're not going to let Minou's father have her, are we?" she asks, her voice husky.

"This is news," Kerry says, looking at me. "Are we?"

"Aren't we obliged to?" I ask. "I mean, this isn't a stray cat we're talking about. Child Protective Services would give her back to her father."

"Not automatically," Kerry points out. "If the kid's afraid of him, CPS will run a criminal check. See what they can turn up."

"See!" Ossie yells. "No one in their right mind would just send her back!"

"Ossie, tell us what Minou is afraid of," Kerry asks.

Ossie plunges her hands in her pockets and shakes off Kerry's arm, moving away from her. "He's a rotten father. After Minou's mom went to jail . . ." her lower lip is trembling and I know this is terribly upsetting to her.

Kerry goes over and hugs her and I can see how hard it is for Ossie not to push her away. But she doesn't. "Tell me what he did then," she urges softly.

Ossie turns so she's looking at me. "He . . . he and some other men were playing cards and I guess he lost a lot of money that he didn't have, so they — the other guys — said that they'd call it square if he gave them Minou."

"If he gave them —" Kerry repeats, shaking her head.

"Gave them Minou," Ossie repeats for her. "They said they were movie producers," she adds contemptuously, "and that they'd make her a child star. Like Jodie Foster in *Taxi Driver*." Ossie gives me an

47

eleven-year-old going on fifty look. "Minou may be just nine but when they asked her to take off her clothes so they could snap some Polaroids, she knew what was up."

"She . . . what did she do?" Kerry asks.

"She told them she had to go to the bathroom and when she was in there with the door locked, she climbed out the window. Then she ran away."

"Smart kid," Kerry mutters.

"Cripes. We need to call the police," I say, feeling ill.

"No," Kerry says, shaking her head. Ossie looks at her in surprised relief.

"No?" I say. "Why no? This is a horrible story."

We hear a thud from upstairs and Kerry looks at Ossie. "Go check on Minou," she says, and Ossie hurries away.

"I don't want Ossie to hear this," she says, coming to sit beside me and lowering her voice. "The police will assume Minou's story is just that — a story. The product of a kid's overwrought imagination. There's no way to verify it. And if the father's around, they may well give her back to him. After all, he is her father."

"Nuts," is all I can think of to say.

Kerry bristles. "What does that mean? You think we should just hand her over?"

I shake my head. "Hardly. But shouldn't we do *something*?" I ask. When she doesn't respond, I try a different tack. "Look, we're all assuming Minou's story is true. What if it's not? What if it really is just what you said — fiction? The product of a kid's imagination. A kid whose mom is in jail and who has to stay with a dad she doesn't know and, okay, maybe doesn't like."

Kerry chews her lip and I can see I'm scoring points.

"The story she told Ossie sounds awful, but to my way of thinking, it's just a little too awful. If we could verify it . . ."

"I know what you're saying," Kerry says wearily. "If dad checks out, we could call him, reunite the two, and wash our hands of Minou. Before CPS opens on Monday morning."

I bristle. "That sounds pretty heartless. What I was *really* thinking was that the kid ought to be with her family. I mean, kids have all sorts of dysfunctional situations — is it our job to pass judgment on them? And with her mom in jail, she needs some stability in her life."

Kerry sighs. "Okay. Coast Investigations could make a couple of phone calls to check out the kid's dad. I'll need my computer. And I'll need to hook into your phone line. " She glances over to see how far along Ossie's gotten with the data entry for my Web page. "Good work for a kid," she nods admiringly. "You know," she says, looking over at the kitchen door, "Ossie seems to identify with Minou for some reason. So let's be gentle with her. And," she searches for the right word, "let's be circumspect. Because if things check out and we send the kid back to her father, Ossie's going to come unglued."

Great. Just great. I groan, and Kerry sees my distress.

"You run the B & B and I'll take care of the Minou problem. Everything will work out," Kerry says soothingly. "It always does."

Try though I might, I can't stifle a small giggle of hysteria.

All things considered, Kerry, Ossie, and I manage to have quite a civilized supper. Earlier, Kerry spent a couple of hours upstairs — ostensibly hooking up and loading programs into Ossie's computer, but actually having a chat with Minou — and she reported back to me that in her opinion the kid was telling the truth. This doesn't please me. For one thing, it means that we'll be stuck with Minou over the weekend, as our only option now seems to be to hang onto her and deliver her to CPS. For another, it means that Minou's father may well be turning over every stone between Nautilus and Lavner Bay looking for the kid, and that makes me uneasy. And despite Kerry's assertion that Minou's story seems credible, I can't quite shed my initial suspicions. Thanks largely to Ossie, however, we manage to talk about other things during the meal.

"Can I take Minou up some supper?" Ossie asks.

"Sure," I tell her and she grabs a plate, spooning a few dabs of pasta and marinara sauce onto it and, after careful consideration, a vole's serving of salad. "Is Minou on a diet?" I ask, making Ossie giggle. "Give her some more, for cripe's sake. And some milk. Don't kids need milk?"

I look at Kerry who shrugs, and I realize she knows as little about kids as I do. And there's no point in asking Ossie who, as I've said, is not normal. She could live quite happily on macaroni dinners and Coke. I mean, her idea of something green with a meal is chocolate chip mint ice cream. No wonder she has such screwy taste in literature and television — her diet is enough to rot anyone's brain.

Kerry clears the table, scraping and rinsing the dishes and putting them in the dishwasher, and I stretch, realizing with satisfaction that the B & B is at seventy-five percent occupancy. Not bad. I really will be able to pay last month's electric bill. And make a dent in the nasty little molehill of debt I've accumulated over the winter, too.

Ossie comes back with an empty plate. "Minou ate everything," she says in amazement. "Even the salad. We started playing a computer game, but she fell asleep. Is she going to be okay?"

I note that she addresses this last question to Kerry.

"Well, does she seem okay?" Kerry asks her. "Does she have bruises? Did she say she was hurt? Is she sneezing or coughing?"

Ossie shakes her head.

"I'm no doctor, but my guess is that she'll be all right."

"I can take care of her," Ossie says, summoning up enough courage to face Allison the Dragon Lady. "You know, make sure she eats, keep her out of your way. Just don't send her back to her father."

I'm a little unnerved. Ossie's usually such a sensible kid but this thing with Minou has really punched her buttons. "Ossie, we can't keep her here forever," I begin reasonably.

51

"Of course not," Ossie says frostily. "But we could keep her until her mother gets out of jail. I mean, it's less than a week."

"It is?" I ask in amazement.

"Uh huh," Ossie says. "Minou says that then her mom will come and get her and they can go home."

Kerry and I exchange looks. "Where's home?" Kerry asks.

Ossie frowns. "I forget. Someplace in Louisiana. Some French name."

"Allison and I will talk about it," Kerry says, and this seems to please Ossie.

"Isn't it your bedtime?" I remind her.

She checks her watch. "*Dark Skies* is on at nine. Mom always lets me watch it in her room. Then I'll go back in with Minou, if that's okay."

Kerry and I agree and Ossie goes off happily, a couple of peanut butter cookies wrapped up in a square of paper towel.

"Is the kid's mom really getting out of jail in a few days?" I ask Kerry.

"This is the first I've heard of it," she says. "But I can check."

I groan, because this brings up a whole new array of possibilities — possibilities I really don't want to consider.

"What's mom in jail for, anyhow?" I ask.

"Theft, according to the kid."

"Hmmm," I reply. "How long do you think Minou's been on the streets?"

Kerry sighs. "A couple of weeks, judging by her clothes and the bathwater."

"Hmmm," I say again. "So, mom's doing time in the county jail? For theft?"

52

Kerry shrugs. "It seems odd, but I guess so." She looks at me strangely. "Why all the questions? What's on your mind?"

"I'm not sure," I tell her. "Something's . . . fishy, though."

"Not that again," Kerry chides. "I thought we agreed the kid's story was true."

"No, you agreed the kid's story was true. Humor me, okay? Let me just talk this out. Does Minou's mom have a name?"

"Yeah. Alyce. Pronounced Ahleez. Like blue cheese. The kid was quite precise about that. Last name is Trudeau. She spelled them both."

"I just wonder . . . if we're not being scammed. Set up for something."

Kerry considers this. "I can't figure out how. Or what. The kid really was in distress when we found her. As for the rest of it — I'll check it out."

I sigh. "I think I'll go upstairs and read. There's some Chardonnay open in the fridge if you like. Oh, and Kerry?"

"Yeah?"

"If you go out, lock up well, okay?"

"I don't plan to go anywhere tonight," she says. Then: "What's wrong, Allison?"

"I don't know," I tell her, "but something is. So let's be careful. And Ker?"

"Yeah?"

"Thanks for being here."

Chapter 7

Something's awakened me and I open my eyes, focusing on a pale, full moon framed by a narrow window. It takes me a moment to remember where I am, and when I do, I swing my legs out of bed and sit in the darkness, listening. And then I hear it again, the noise that awakened me — a kind of shuffling scrape. It seems to be coming from the deck one story below my bedroom window and I hunt around in the dark for my sneakers, tying them by feel. Pulling a sweatshirt over my head, I grab the Mag Light I keep just inside the door of my room in

case of power outages and step out onto the landing.
The stairs creak a little as I descend and at Ossie's
room, I open the door slowly, shining the light on
the bed. Two heads — one blonde and one brunette —
and one pair of glowing cat's eyes. Sammy's taken to
sleeping with Ossie, which is okay with me because
he farts under the covers. Ossie hasn't complained
about this, and her silence on the subject makes me
believe that for some mysterious feline reason, Sam's
on his best behavior with her. Who can figure cats?
So everything seems okay here. I continue down the
stairs into the lobby, across the floor, and into the
kitchen, flipping on the light beside the back door. It
illuminates the yard, showing me very clearly that
there's nothing out there. No wandering guests
who've stayed out late and forgotten to ask for a key
in advance. Still, I unlock the back door anyhow and
step outside. Just to be sure.

The first thing that hits me is what a pretty
night it is — a full moon low in the sky, trailing
wisps of clouds like smoke. The second thing that
hits me is the smell of cigarettes. More precisely, a
cigarette, which is right there, practically under my
feet. I bend to pick it up. It's only half-smoked, and
its still-burning end glows red in the dark. The hair
rises on the back of my neck — what's going on here?
There's a sign on the registration desk clearly stating
that the B & B is a non-smoking establishment. So
that means what — that one of the guests was out
here clandestinely puffing and tossed the cigarette
when she heard me coming? If so, where did she go
and why didn't I hear her?

There is, however, another possibility, a more
unsettling one. Maybe the smoker isn't one of the

guests at all. Maybe it's someone else, someone I interrupted with my arrival, someone I really don't want to meet. I'm thinking hard about this, wondering what I ought to do, so when the kitchen door opens behind me, I almost leap out of my shorts.

"Oh, it's you," says Kerry, relief in her voice. "I thought something was wrong."

"It is," I say softly. "I heard noises. When I came out onto the deck I found this." I hold up the cigarette for her inspection.

She whistles softly. "Not good. Whichever one of your guests tossed that baby could have burned this place down."

"Yes, they could have, but maybe it wasn't a guest, Kerry," I say, my teeth starting to chatter, as much from anxiety as from the cold night air. "Even a clandestine smoker would've put this out."

"Who then?" she asks, looking past me down the deck, then back behind her.

I'm tired of holding the stupid cigarette between my fingers so I step on it, grinding it out. "That's what I'm wondering. A burglar?"

She shakes her head. "No way. I've never heard of a burglar this dumb."

"Let's go inside," I say. "I want to put some more clothes on, then go back out and take a look around."

She shakes her head again. "Bad idea. You'll just stumble around in the dark. Remember the bear."

I blush, because I do indeed remember the bear. Last winter, just before Thanksgiving, Kerry had come over for dinner and we were sitting up late in the kitchen, drinking coffee and yakking about nothing, when a horrendous crash and a house-jarring thud occurred outside. I ran out onto the back deck, flipping on lights and cursing loudly, only to see a large, black-furred, fat-bottomed bear sitting in the moonlight not ten feet from the house. He seemed not at all perturbed by the noise and lights, but glanced back once over his shoulder, whuffed, and returned to his meal — a suet ball which I had put out for the birds. Hey, I didn't mind his having a little late-night snack in the moonlight. What I *did* mind, however, was the wreckage of my expensive bird-feeding station which I had ordered from a chichi catalogue catering to wild birds and the women who love them. The wreckage of five feeders lay around him and I felt myself doing a slow burn.

"You fat-assed sonofabitch!" I yelled.

"Whuff," he replied, licking suet off nine-inch nails.

"Holy shit," Kerry whispered, clutching me, peering over my shoulder. "It's a bear," she croaked, stating the obvious.

"No shit, Sherlock," I said, not bothering to keep my voice down. "So what do we do?" I must admit, that last snort of coffee with Bailey's was making me bolder than I would otherwise have been.

"I don't know," she whispered feebly.

"You don't know? You're an Indian, for cripe's sake — you should know. Shouldn't we pray or chant or sacrifice something?"

"I'm going to pee my pants. Let's just go back inside. Quietly and slowly. We wouldn't want to disturb him."

"Hell no," I said indignantly. "Let's not disturb him. He's just demolished a hundred dollars' worth of bird feeders I ordered in a moment of weakness from some overpriced nature catalogue. But let's not disturb him."

Kerry grabbed me by the neck of my sweatshirt and hauled me back inside. "Enough about your bird feeders. You're ranting. Be quiet. When he's done, he'll go away."

Of course, he did. That night. But he returned the next night and the night after that and the night after that, no doubt responding to the memory of that delicious suet ball drawing him back like a addict in search of a fix. Night after night we had to endure an ursine soliloquy of moans, snorts, and huffs as the fur-bearing hulk protested the absence of his nocturnal nosh, the across-the chalkboard rasp of those astonishing nails as he vented his frustration on the deck railing from which the aforementioned treat had hung and, finally, the creak and snap of two-by-fours as he collapsed against our fence one night in a fit of famished anguish. I mean, this wasn't just a bear, this was a performer, a diva among bears, an Oscar wannabe, a veritable Brunhilde. And if she (or he) hadn't been so fucking destructive, I might have been amused.

In search of advice, I called the state office of Fish and Wildlife, whereupon a sympathetic state employee named Tammy sent me a brochure entitled "Living Happily With Bears." Oh goody. What I'd had in mind was living happily without bears. Next, I called our local constabulary, producing a good belly laugh from the Chief of Police, who informed me that that particular bear was, like a local juvenile delinquent, a frequent offender.

"Yes, ma'am, we know him real well," the Chief

told me in a confiding voice. "He's been in trouble before."

"I don't want to know his rap sheet," I said icily, "I want to know how to make him go away."

"Lady, there's not a thing you can do," the voice of the law told me. "That bear'll go when he's good and ready. You see, he's stocking up for winter. Yes, ma'am, that's what he's doing. But I have to admit this has been one of his bad nights — we've had calls from all over the place. Why, the folks across from Hamburger Heaven just called to say he was in the dumpster. They were laughing — didn't bother them. So don't you worry your head about this. He'll be gone soon enough."

All of this condescending claptrap did nothing to reassure me, but sure enough, one night Brunhilde just didn't show up. That night became two, then a week, then two, and I figured that at last, we were bearless. Nevertheless, long after her nocturnal visits, it was months before I hung out another bird feeder, and much longer than that before I'd felt really safe sitting out on the back deck looking at the moon.

"Earth to Allison," Kerry says, recalling me from my own private rerun of *Wild America*.

"Huh?"

"I was saying that my guess is whoever you surprised is long gone. I'll take a look at the doors and windows first thing tomorrow before the guests get up. In the meantime," she bends to pick up the cigarette, "let's go back to bed. It wouldn't hurt to leave the yard light on. And maybe turn some more lights on out front, too."

I close and lock the back door while Kerry finds a plastic bag for the cigarette. "Unfiltered Camel," she

59

says with distaste. "Almost no one smokes these things anymore." On her way out of the kitchen, she pauses, realizing I'm not following her.

"Allison?"

"Yeah, yeah," I say. "I think I'll just sit here in the kitchen for a while and worry."

"Suit yourself," she says. "Just don't go wandering around in the dark checking out noises by yourself, okay? Come and get me. Better yet, call the cops."

I sit in the kitchen for a long time, listening to the house noises, thinking about bears and burglars. To my relief, nothing happens. About four-thirty I make a cup of tea and as I drink it, I wonder if the shenanigans on the deck a few hours ago could be related to Minou's arrival. Coincidence? The mystery writers whose wares I sell opine that there is no such thing as coincidence. I think about this for a bit, trying to connect the dots. If the cigarette didn't belong to one of the guests — and I doubt it did given that my yuppie clientele probably didn't smoke unfiltered Camels — then it belonged to someone else. And if it belonged to someone else connected with Minou, who was that someone else? It wasn't the kid — she's upstairs asleep. It wasn't the mother — she's in the county jail. It wasn't the father — he's languishing in Nautilus, apparently, and even if he has slouched his way down the coast, he couldn't possibly know where Minou is. So who does that leave — the so-called movie producers? I snort. Hardly. Then who? Someone casing the B & B for future burglary? I doubted it. Kids trying to break in and grab what they could, and take off? Maybe. And with that, I come to the end of the possibilities my sluggish brain can provide. I lean back in my chair, thinking about nada and at five-forty, the sky begins to lighten. At five fifty-nine the sun comes up, freeing me from my self-appointed vigil. I pass Kerry on the stairs and she's clearly surprised to see me. "You're an apparition," she says critically. "Better go to bed. You'll scare even Sammy dressed like that."

I look down, realizing that I'm still in my green plaid flannel shorts, blue sweatshirt, and beat-up Nikes. "Hmmph," I say as I continue on up the stairs. I intend to think about the cigarette a little more, but when I reach my room, I fall onto the bed, exhausted, and I'm asleep before I can take my shoes off.

Chapter 8

By ten a.m., the collective noises of the B & B have awakened me — toilets flushing, the groan of a troublesome water pipe, feet on stairs, doors opening and closing, car engines starting, voices outside. I toss my clothes in the corner and stagger into the shower, leaning against the tile wall for a few minutes while the water splashes on my feet. Once I think I'm sufficiently conscious not to drown, I soap and shampoo, shut off the water (it's getting cold anyhow) and step out, grabbing a towel. I swipe at the steam on the bathroom mirror, looking at the woman looking back at me. She's red-haired, freckle-faced, and solemn. I try a smile. Better. Sighing, I realize that I don't smile enough these days — in fact, I can't recall the last time I was, well, really excited about something. Thinking hard, I finally dredge a happy event from the wastebasket of memory: a bookscouting trip I made last year to Los Angeles, about three months before I came north to Oregon.

I had bet my friend Bradley that I could make enough money in an afternoon of buying and selling first editions to take us to dinner at the best restaurant in West Hollywood. And I did. With Brad in tow, we hit a Goodwill store where only half an hour of searching among stacks of donated books produced two treasures: a copy of Tim Powers' *Dinner at the Deviant's Palace,* complete with bookjacket, in excellent condition; and a copy of *Green Eyes* by Lucius Shepard, with, alas, no jacket, but still in pretty good shape. I had a customer who, I knew, would swoon at the prospect of acquiring the Powers book, so if I had no luck selling it, I knew where it could find a home. There was a nice paperback collection of Jack Vance's *Worlds of Adventure* series, but I passed it up — paperbacks are just too iffy. I got both the Powers and the Shepard books for five dollars total, so I left the Goodwill store feeling terrific. And several hours and several used bookstores later, I was a hundred and twelve dollars richer. It's easy if you know how.

Sighing again, I brush my teeth and blow-dry my hair, wondering if I really like my locks *au naturel*. Until just a few months ago, I covered up my very red hair with a garnet dye job. I can't really say why I chose garnet — maybe because it's in the same family as red? For years I'd had to put up with being called "Carrot Top," "Rusty," "Red," and other less-than-clever names. As soon as I left home for college, I donned my garnet disguise. I must say that provoked just as many stares but not one rude name. Well, there was the little old lady in the supermarket in Lancaster one Sunday who muttered "punk" under her breath but I wasn't sure if she was offended by my hair, my clothes (which were black) or my attitude (which was, admittedly, surly). And now? Who was I now? Someone who was tired of garnet, evidently.

"That's Ms. Red to you, buster," I say belligerently, practicing my answer to the wise-guy gas station attendants and grocery baggers of this world.

"Merrrrr," whines Sammy, pushing open the bathroom door, startling me. He follows me into the bedroom where I pull on a pair of clean jeans, purple socks and Birkenstocks, a T-shirt, and a pretty purple, teal, and gold plaid shirt. Flannel, of course. "What's up?" I ask Sammy. "You couldn't persuade Kerry to feed you?" He butts his head urgently against my leg. "C'mon, hairbag. Let's go downstairs before you starve to death. Me too, for that matter."

Descending the stairs, I realize that I feel a little spacey. Too many hours spent fretting in the dark and too little sleep will do it to you every time.

I peek into Ossie's room but it's empty, bed neatly made, new computer sitting idle on a table against the window. I look around at the walls, which Ossie has decorated with a poster advertising the Star Trek movie about the whales, and another one for *The X-Files.* THE TRUTH IS OUT THERE, this poster reads. Oh yeah? I remind myself that Ossie's interest in the paranormal and the out-of-this-world isn't really unusual for a kid who believes that her father and brothers were abducted by aliens. After all, when you consider what Pan assures me is the truth — that her husband ran out on her, taking her three sons but leaving Ossie — I too might choose to believe in alien abduction. At least it leaves you with hope.

There's no one in the lobby, no one in the kitchen, and no one on the deck. In fact, the B & B is deserted. What's up, I wonder. Maybe Ossie is right. Maybe there is something to this alien abduction theory after all. I fill Sammy's kibble bowl, change his water, put some coffee on, throw a bagel in the microwave, and am just sitting down with the newspaper when there are footsteps on the deck. Laughing, Ossie and Minou come in the back door, and Ossie hangs up her jacket, shaking Minou's shoulder, motioning for her to do the same. But the kid is transfixed, looking at me.

"Hi," I say reassuringly. "I'm Allison, remember?"

The kid looks back at me with approximately the same enthusiasm a mouse might regard a rattler.

"Say hi," Ossie coaches.

"Hi," the kid says tentatively.

"I won't bite," I tell her, instantly regretting the bad thoughts I've been having about her. Because she's pathetic. Oh, she's clean and dressed in decent but too-big clothes of Ossie's, but her hair has been chopped off any old way, her nails are bitten to the quick, and her huge brown eyes are filled with alarm. The kid's a disaster.

"Allison owns this place," Ossie explains.

If it's possible, Minou's eyes get bigger. "You do? All of it?"

"Last time I looked."

She cocks her head on one side. "But you're a girl," she says, chomping a nail, evidently trying to digest the two seemingly incompatible facts of femaleness and business ownership.

"So?" I ask, not exactly happy to have to play Socrates before my morning coffee.

"Well, um, where, um, *Maman* and I stayed in Nautilus there were, like, cabins," she says, writhing with the sheer, horrible effort of getting all these words out. "But a man owned them," she ends abruptly.

"Women can own cabins, too," I assure her.

"Oh," she says, taking a pause from her fingernails. Then she asks, "Are you a grown-up?"

I burst out laughing. "Yeah. For quite a few years now."

"Oh," she says again.

I look at my watch. "Want to make some lunch?" I ask Ossie.

She looks suspicious, no doubt anticipating my insistence that she eat something green. "Like what?"

"Oh, like macaroni and cheese from the blue box. I bet Minou would like that. She could even help you." And I could hang around and ask questions. I guess I'm somewhat surprised that Minou is as receptive to questions as she is, so maybe I'll play sleuth. Heck, the worst that can happen is that she'll refuse to answer.

"Okay," Ossie tells me with a grin, plainly relieved that I'm not insisting on the consumption of loathsome veggies. "C'mon, Minou," she says and the kid trails after her into the pantry.

"So where's Kerry?" I call to Ossie.

"She went into Nautilus," Ossie yells. "She said she'd be back just after lunch."

While Ossie pours water in a pot and puts it on the stove, Minou stands by her elbow, transfixed.

"Haven't you ever done this?" Ossie asks her.

She shakes her head.

"Hmmf," Ossie says, handing her a measuring cup. "Go to the fridge and get out the milk. Then pour a quarter cup of milk into this cup. See, it'll have to come up to this mark, here."

"So, Minou," I say with about as much finesse as a two-by-four, "why were you and your mother living in those cabins? Were you just new in town?"

She puts the quart of milk down on the table and looks at me once, quickly, over the top. "Uh huh," she says. "*Maman* and me, we're from Trudeau. That's in Louisiana. All my mom's family live there. Our name is the same name as the town," she says proudly.

"That's nice. What about your dad?"

"Him!" she says scornfully. "He's from nowhere, *Maman* says."

"Sounds as though your mother is mad at your dad," I venture.

Minou nods, agreeing. "She says he's no good. Nothing but trouble. We don't even have his name. His is LaPlante." She looks at me in disgust. "There's no town named LaPlante."

"So how come you were living with him? What happened to your mom? That must be quite a story."

She sighs, apparently agreeable to telling it. "We were living in Trudeau. We were doing okay, staying with *Tante* Marie. But he called one night and told *Maman* that he had a good job up here, and a house, and that he was all straightened out. So we left Trudeau. He even said he had a cat for me," she adds softly, bitterness and disappointment in her voice. I feel guilty all over again because either she's the best little actress in the world or this is true. "We left home and rode all the way up here on the bus, and he didn't have a house at all. Or a job. Or a cat, either."

"Why did he say those things, Minou? Did your mother tell you?"

The kid nods, macaroni and cheese forgotten. "She said he needed someone to take care of him, to put a roof over his head while he gambled. She said she should have known better and that she wasn't going to do it again." The question that arises in my mind was why she did it in the first place but, as the wags say, that's another conversation.

"I can see why she was mad at him."

"Uh huh. They had a big fight at the bus station, right on the sidewalk. It went on for a long time. Finally *Maman* took me and we walked a long ways and she got us — her and me — a cabin. It was kind of fun. *Maman* got a job in a restaurant right beside the cabins and she used to bring me stuff home — hamburgers, fries. It was cool."

"How long did you stay there, Minou? With your mom? Can you remember?"

She scrunches her face in thought. "Four of *Maman*'s paydays. She said we'd be moving into a trailer soon, and that we'd save our money so we could go home. And then *he* showed up one night. I asked *Maman* how he knew where we were, but she just sent me to the store for some Cokes. When I got back, *he* was lying on the bed watching tv, looking all smiley." She looks up at me. "I knew they'd been having sex."

I almost choke on my bagel. Out of the mouths of babes.

"How *did* he know where we were?" she asks me.

I shake my head, not wanting to give her the obvious answer: her mom told him.

She gives an angry shrug. "He started . . . hanging around. At first he'd come over when she got off work and she'd send me out for ice cream." She rolls her eyes. "Like I didn't know what was happening. And then he'd come over when he knew she was working." A little warning rocket went up in my brain. "He started really trying to be friendly with me — you know, bringing me stuff. He took me to a couple movies, too." She falls silent, clearly remembering things that cause her pain and I feel like a rat, but I need to know.

"How did your mother get sent to jail, Minou?"

She looks up, a plea for understanding in her eyes. "It was my fault," she says. "*Maman* just got paid. We walked to the bank to cash her check. She had a headache and wanted to go back to the cabin and lie down so she gave me a dollar for an ice cream cone and all the rent money to take to the manager. I should have gone straight there, but I went to the store first and got the ice cream cone. When I started walking back, *he* was there in the driveway. My father. He knew I had the money!" she wailed. "How did he know that? He said the cabin

69

manager would think I stole it and that an adult needed to pay. I didn't believe him. I shouldn't have given him the money. I didn't want to. But he made me." She looks up at me. "He grabbed my arm and shook it. He hurt me."

"It's okay," I tell her, appalled. "There was nothing you could have done."

She shakes her head. "I should have . . . kicked him. Or yelled. Or something."

"Minou, it wasn't your fault," I tell her. "What happened then?"

"I went back to the room and told *Maman* what happened, that *he* took the money because he said an adult needed to pay the cabin man. She didn't say anything, just got up and went out. She was gone a long time and when she came back, she acted . . . funny."

"What kind of funny? Was she angry?"

"Not mad. Kind of sad. She said she'd taken care of the cabin rent for the next couple of days and that I could stay there and I wasn't supposed to worry. Then she wrote a note and put it and some money in an envelope and told me to put my things in a bag and go over to the restaurant where she worked and give the note to the lady there. I did that and the lady made me a burger and pretty soon the police came and took *Maman* away," Minou says, tears in her eyes. "I didn't even get to talk to her. The nice lady in the restaurant — she works there, she's *Maman*'s friend — says the police took her away because she stole something and sold it for money."

"I'm sorry," I told her. "And then what? You and your father stayed on at the cabin for awhile?"

She shakes her head. "No. That afternoon he

brought those men over and they played cards. That's when I ran away."

"Macaroni's done," Ossie says, rescuing us from this horrible story with a dose of practicality. "You can bring the milk over."

Minou does so and Ossie resumes her lesson. "You drain the macaroni, see, and pour in the milk. Then you rip open this packet of cheese stuff — here, you do it — and add it to the milk and macaroni. Then you mix it up." Ossie hands Minou a spoon and the younger girl dutifully stirs. "Make sure you get all the orange stuff mixed in," Ossie says.

"What was your mother's friend's name?" I ask Minou. "The one who she worked with."

"Juanita," Minou says. "Why?"

"I don't know — I'd just like to go and talk to her," I reply. "Seems like your mom got a bum rap."

"It was all *his* fault," she says and I'm astonished at the bitterness in her voice. "Why didn't he leave us alone? Why did he call us in Trudeau? Why did *Maman* listen to him? And when she found out he lied to her, why did she let him come around?"

I sigh, pretty sure that I know the real reason that he didn't leave them alone — because Minou's mom didn't want him to. My opinion of the fair Alyce — low when Minou started this tale — is considerably lower now. What kind of a spineless worm is she?

"Oh well," Minou says, her dark mood gone. "*Maman* will be out of jail next week. Then we can go home."

That's certainly good news, but before I explore it, I want to keep her talking about her father and the movie producers. "That was pretty smart of you

71

to jump out the window when the bad guys let you go the bathroom," I tell her.

She smiles shyly. "I saw it in a movie."

Hearing a noise in the front of the house, Ossie hurries out of the kitchen. "Kerry's back," she tells me happily bouncing back in. "We're going to go take some photos later," she informs me. "Of Swimming Cat Cove." When I don't leap up and down with excitement, she reminds me why I ought to be thrilled. "For your Web page," she says in disapproval. "You remember, don't you?"

"Oh yeah, the Web page," I reply, realizing that indeed I have forgotten about it in all the excitement of the cigarette smoker from the night before. "Cool."

Ossie flashes me a give-me-strength look, ancient, dweebish fossil that I am, and turns her adoring gaze back to Kerry.

"I brought us some lunch," Kerry says, unpacking Chinese food. "Moo shu vegetables for Allison and me. And noodles."

"Yuk," says Ossie, dividing the macaroni into two bowls.

"Quiet, shorty," Kerry tells her. "You're probably going to die of malnutrition. However, if by some fluke you survive, you're bound to develop deficient brain cells that won't let you do anything more challenging than operate a B & B. Your career as a silicon guru may never materialize."

Ossie looks at her in some concern. "Yeah?"

"Yeah. So you're going to have to eat vegetables. Not these," she explains, "because these are my lunch. But something. And soon."

"Okay," Ossie says in a small voice. "I will."

"Some fish wouldn't hurt either," Kerry says, pressing her luck. "Brain food, you know."

"Can we take our lunch outside," Ossie asks me.

"Sure. Just remember to bring the dishes back in. And rinse them before you put them in the dishwasher. Even silicon gurus have to attend to household chores."

"So what's up?" I ask Kerry. "Did you prowl around outside this morning?"

She shrugs. "Yeah. But I didn't find anything that would explain last night's cigarette."

"Oh well. Maybe it wasn't anything more mysterious than one of the guests out for a forbidden nocturnal puff."

"Hmmm," she says, clearly not in agreement. Sitting down opposite me at the table, she dishes up our lunch.

"So what did you turn up in Nautilus?"

She chews thoughtfully, pours some Perrier, and frowns. "Well, for starters Minou's mom is not going to be released next week — that's wishful thinking on someone's part. Alyce's bail hearing's on Tuesday." She gives me a baleful look. "And in my opinion, no way will she be released even if she could find someone willing to post bail."

"No? Why not?"

"Think about it," she says, ticking the points off on her fingers. "She's from out of state, true, she has a job, but it's a crummy one, she's living in a pay-by-the-week cabin, she has no ties to the community, and then there's that deadbeat husband of hers who could talk her into taking off for Nome or anywhere."

"But she has Minou."

"So?" Kerry shrugs. "Kids are portable. Look how easily Alyce transported her up here."

"What about Minou's story — that her dad lost her in a card game to the movie producers when she was left alone with him. Wouldn't that influence the court?"

Kerry laughs and I'm sorry I asked the question.

"Kerry, do you really believe Minou?"

She considers this. "Yeah, I do. But it doesn't matter, does it? If what she claims is true — and I'll try to verify that by getting the father's rap sheet — then theoretically she's in danger because he'll be looking for her. But he won't find her because we've got her and intend to deliver her to CPS on Monday. That's tomorrow, incidentally. She'll be fostered out by CPS while her mom does time in Salem. And if her story isn't true, she'll still be fostered out. Right?" She gives me an appraising look. "Why all this interest in whether the kid's story is true or not? I thought you just wanted her out of here?"

"Don't start with me," I warn her. "Like I said, let me just talk this out."

Kerry groans. "You're not still worried about a scam, are you? I mean, the kid will be out of here tomorrow morning."

I give her a glare. "What did Alyce steal, anyhow?"

"One of those new digital cameras. Very portable unfortunately. And very expensive. Then she went straight to the local pawn shop."

"How did she get caught?"

"The pawn shop owner got suspicious. Called the cops." Kerry takes a few more bites of lunch, delicately wiping her lips with a paper napkin. "She's looking at a year and a half in the women's prison in Salem. This is felony theft we're talking about. The owner of the shop where she lifted the camera naturally wants to press charges."

My appetite flees. "God dammit all to hell," I yell, heedless of who hears. "What a mess." I think for a minute, mulling over Minou's story. I guess I believe it — I mean the kid seems so sincere. And Kerry's probably right — it doesn't matter to the kid's safety whether the story is true or not. But still, there's something nagging at me. "You know, maybe we need to go ask some questions at the place where Minou and her mom were staying. The kid said Alyce wrote a note and put some money in an envelope. What was that for, do you suppose?"

"Beats me. Where is this place, anyhow?"

"Let's see — a bunch of little cabins just off Highway 101. There's a coffee shop pretty close by. Oh, and the kid said it's just around the corner from an orange motel with a big penny on the roof."

Kerry shudders. "I think I know the street. If it's where I think it is, it's a real fleabag."

"I could drive into Nautilus and take a look at the place," I say. "Maybe talk to Alyce's co-worker."

"Talk to who?" Kerry asks, mystified.

"Ha," I say smugly.

"I thought I was the PI," she says, mopping up the last of the Chinese food. "How'd you find out all this stuff?"

"Don't worry, your license is safe. The kid just wanted to talk, I guess. And, evil person that I am, I encouraged her childish babbling."

Kerry raises a eyebrow. "What's really on your

mind, Allison? Could it be you're thawing? Has the kid gotten to you?"

"Give me a break. I'm hardly Cruella de Vil — you know that. Anyhow, I don't have anything else to do this afternoon — no toilets to clean, no laundry to do. A trip to Nautilus could be quite salutary."

Kerry makes a rude noise. "Are you asking me to watch the desk?"

"Uh huh."

"I'll watch it. Go, already."

"Oh, and Kerry?"

"Mmmm?"

"Maybe you could use one of your computer programs to find the aunt that Minou told me about. First name Marie. Last name Trudeau. In —"

"I know. Trudeau, Louisiana. I can probably do that but why on earth would you want me to?"

"Tell you later," I say, and saunter out the door.

Chapter 9

I've left Kerry busy at her laptop, personing the reception desk, and I'm zooming down the highway toward Nautilus. Hey, how hard can it be to find the right Trudeaus? Kerry once bragged that with her on-line phone book and maps not only could she find anyone, anywhere, but she could zero in on the street where they lived. Sounds a little unlikely to me, but I have an idea that the information might be useful.

What's the real story about the kid's dad, I wonder. Is he truly the rat Minou says he is? As credible as she seems, I must admit that I'm having

trouble believing he sold her to the Angelinos. What's
the going price for a kid these days, anyway? And
why do I care? Well, for one reason, I love a good
story . . . and this one just doesn't hang together. Who
told Minou that her mother was getting out of jail on
Tuesday? What was in the envelope for Juanita? Why
was Minou really living behind Safeway? And why
didn't the kid seem more, well, upset? And for
another reason, yeah, maybe I am thawing a little. I
may not completely believe the kid's story, but she's
the undeniable victim in this drama. Dad may have a
gambling problem, and mom may be a thief, but each
of them chose to do what they did. Minou's too
young to choose her fate.

So, even though there are weighty matters
hanging over my head, so to speak, I'm feeling unaccountably optimistic. Maybe it's the blue sky or the
foamy wavelets breaking on the beach or the smells
of cedar or pine or fir or the gulls surfing the air
currents, cackling now and then as if one of them
had told a joke. I can't explain it — it's a coastal
thing. And it pulls folks here every summer in flocks.
Even the lucky ones, those who have parallel-parked
their seven-person mini-vans in sheetrocked suburbia
complete with security gates and no sidewalks, feel
the need to chuck it all from time to time and do
the coastal thing. Why this primal need to get sand
between your toes and stare at the ocean until you
spaz out? Beats me. But I'm counting on the phe-
nomenon repeating itself this summer.

And speaking of summer, I see now how it truly
is Nature's gift to us here in Oregon. Having suffered
through the Winter From Hell, with record rainfall,
record winds, and record destruction, I am almost

ready to give my firstborn (sorry, Sammy) as an offering to the sun god. Anything to make dry, calm, warmth continue.

A horn honks behind me and I sigh, pulling into a state park from my place in line behind a flatulent sedan from Minnesota. Once parked, I get out to stare at the ocean and finish the latte I picked up on my way through Windsock. Heck, I'm just the same as anyone else — give me an ocean and I'll stare at it. So I'm sipping and staring, thinking again about how terrific summer really is here in the upper left-hand corner of the map, when I hear a happy voice hailing me.

"Hi there!"

I turn and it's Eve, the smiley half of the Eve and Katherine Show. As usual, she looks as though the world was made today, just for her, and damn if she isn't pleased with it. I scan the area for the dour Katherine and Eve grins even more broadly, if that's possible. I wonder idly if her teeth are crowned because they look so perfect and white and which anti-depressant she's on.

"So, how are you enjoying the coast?" I ask inanely because it's evident that she's as tickled as a clam in broth.

"It's fabulous," she declares, planting herself beside me on the picnic table. We sit in awkward silence for a moment before Eve turns to me and says, "You know, I really don't want to climb Everest or sail the Pacific single-handed. Kath was just saying that to . . . embarrass me."

"Mmmm," I reply, recalling their conversation of yesterday, wishing myself away from here. Now I'm supposed to ask why and dammit, I don't want to.

Instead I opt for inscrutable silence which surprises me even more than it does Eve.

"You see," she says after another mutually uncomfortable moment, "the thing of it is that, well, we're about ready to go our own ways."

I shift uneasily and Eve must sense my distress.

"I'm only telling you this so you don't think I'm a total bimbo," she says. "I love what I've seen of the coast and I really would like to own a B & B here. I have capital to invest and I think this might just be the place to do it. I'm serious. Really serious."

I groan, feeling genuinely sorry for her. "Eve, you need to spend a winter here," I tell her. "Put your money in a nice, safe mutual fund, get a job at a motel cleaning toilets, and see how serious you are after storm season."

She vaults off the picnic table and brushes off the seat of her pants. "You make it sound . . . horrendous. Like you have typhoons. It can't be that bad."

I burst out laughing, vividly recalling the Night of the Big Blow when wooden shingles went sailing from the B & B's roof like jet-propelled frisbees and our metal woodshed was ripped from its moorings and delivered to a vacant (thank you, God) lot on the other side of 101. "It can be that bad," I assure her. "It will be that bad. Go to the library and read back issues of *The Oregonian* if you don't believe me. Ask people. You'll find out I'm telling the truth."

"But why do people *stay* if the weather is so bad for so much of the year?" she asks, clearly trying to understand.

I finish my latte and crumple the cup into a ball. "Why? I guess because it suits us." I'm amazed to hear myself saying this. "Maybe we're perverse. Maybe it's the contrast between terrible and wonderful. I can't explain it to you. But if . . . heck, not if, *when* I decide to do something else besides the B & B, I'm going to stay. Here, I mean."

"*You'd* stay?" she asks, clearly shocked. "But from the way you talked, I thought you hated it. The storms and all."

I ponder this. "Yes and no. If I wasn't constantly worried about my roof being ripped off and deposited in backyards from Windsock to Nautilus, I might be better able to appreciate the coast's charms." And of course there's the worry of being responsible for other people — Aunt Grace's legacy to me. But I can hardly tell Eve about that. Come to think of it, how can I tell any prospective buyer about that? So I shrug. "I think I'm just too young to have this kind of responsibility," I say. "Or else I'm temperamentally unsuited for it. I know I'd be happier with my nose buried in my books. Literally. And I can run my book business from anywhere, so . . ." I shrug again. "I haven't given this a tremendous amount of thought, but there's nothing particularly appealing about where I came from — Lancaster, California," I tell her. "Like I said, one of the armpits of the world."

She nods, then gives me a chagrined smile. "You wouldn't be interested in handing over your toilets to someone, would you? Because I've looked up and down the coast and I like it here. Right here. In soggy Lavner Bay."

I turn to her, realizing what she's offering me — a way out. Right here in front of my eyes I have A Prospective Buyer. Yikes. This changes everything.

Suddenly Eve's beaming smiles, her interest in me, her offbeat screwiness seems understandable. A buyer! Be cool, I tell myself, frantically trying to recall just what I said to Eve yesterday when she found me on the deck and started grilling me about the B & B. As I recall, I didn't say much except that I disliked cleaning toilets and thought I'd be better off selling books. Which is pretty much the same thing I've said today. So even if I haven't been enthusiastic, at least I've been consistent.

"I don't recall mentioning that Lavner Bay B & B is for sale," I say coyly, which is a pretty lame opening gambit even if it is the truth. With apologies to Sam, better to call a spade a spade.

"No, *you* didn't mention it."

"What?" I'm shocked. "You mean someone else did?"

"Yeah. Sort of. Kaye at The Daily Grind hinted that you might, just might, mind you, be interested in selling and that it wouldn't hurt to ask."

I'm beyond shocked. I'm . . . flabbergasted. And pissed off, too. And then I rein myself in. What's to be pissed off about? It wasn't as though I told Kaye secrets which, if revealed, could mean the end of life as we know it. Heck, all I did was tell her the truth — that I was thinking of selling. And she did mention to me that there had been a couple of women into the coffee house lately, sipping espresso and chatting, talking about buying a coastal business. I just didn't connect them with Eve and Katherine. The Daily Grind is the AP or UPI of Windsock — dozens of pairs of women pass through there every week in the summer, and at least half of them are interested in moving to the coast, and half of that half are interested in starting a business and begin their inquiries there. So I didn't take what she said too seriously. But I guess I should have.

So, fate has dropped A Potential Buyer in my lap. Now what? I clear my throat, ready to make a pronouncement. But Eve beats me to it.

"Are you interested?" she asks.

So, here it is. The Big Question. And I'm amazed to find myself hesitating, dammit. For about three seconds. Then the prospect of not having to worry about the roof, Brunhilde, my occupancy rate and, yes, the toilets, exerts its siren call and I manage a cool "I could be. For the right person. And the right price."

"Terrific!" Eve beams even more broadly if that's possible. "Can we talk? Now?"

I shake my head. "No. I have some pressing business in Nautilus. We can talk when I get back. I'll get my financial records together. Let's say this evening?"

She's almost jumping up and down in her eagerness and as she bounds off to her car, I shake my head in guilty dismay. What would Aunt Grace say?

Chapter 10

The Bide-a-Wee Cabins are just off 101, directly around the corner from the orange Penny Pincher Motel whose roof is, indeed, adorned with a hideous replica of a one-cent piece. I guess its sheer ugliness has kept me from noticing it before. Not that the Bide-a-Wee cabins are anything to get excited about, either. There are eleven cabins and judging from the tattered curtains and general air of decrepitude the place exudes, a wee is about the length of time anyone would want to bide in them. Sure enough, there's a coffee shop on the same piece of real estate as the Bide, painted the same nondescript gray as the cabins, so I surmise that it must be in this eatery where the fair Alyce once worked. Feeling depressed, I park on the street and trudge across the dusty gravel parking lot. Some folks' downward mobility amazes me. I mean, couldn't Alyce have done better for herself? If she had to sling hash for a living, couldn't it have been quality hash? I, too, have had to resort to waiting tables in my time, but I would sooner have walked dogs than worked here. I know for a fact that the Golden Arches just down the street always has a sign out advertising their need for warm bodies to fulfill the McUrges of tourists. And they pay more than minimum wage, too.

Inside, I discover the eatery has a name — The Grile, a fascinating etymological amalgam of *grill* and *grille* — and that it's about the size of the average walk-in closet. Which is to say there is enough room for a grill (or is that a grile?), a counter with nine stools (all topped with possibly the original fifties' red vinyl, three of them repaired with gray duct tape) and a cash register. And a woman with an improbably black, old-fashioned bouffant hairdo as wide as her hips, a pink nylon uniform too tight across her, um, chest, and a ferocious frown. Her name tag says JUANITA. Bingo.

I look around for a menu and seeing none, make the mistake of asking, "What's good?"

She eyes me as though I've committed the social gaffe of the century. "Nothin'," she replies.

"Oh," I say, undeterred. "In that case, I'll have some coffee."

She gives me a speculative look and pours me a cup of coffee the color and consistency of molasses.

"Can I have some milk with this?" I ask, dismayed that I might actually have to drink this mess.

"Gosh, I didn't get out to milk the cows this mornin'," she says, leaning one ample hip against the grill. "Waddya really want?"

"Alyce," I say, realizing that the last time anyone put anything over on Juanita was probably the turn of the century. "Minou's mother. I'm a friend. The kid's in trouble. She told me they stayed here."

She looks at me speculatively. "I don't know no Ah-leez," she says, scribbling on her order pad. "Here's a bill for your coffee. I got work to do in the back. Now get lost."

I feel my cheeks flame red and bite back several pithy replies that come to mind. Does Kerry have to take this abuse as she plies her trade on the mean streets of Nautilus? This PI business sucks. Digging a dollar out of my jeans, I fling it on the counter and am halfway across the parking lot before I realize I'm still clutching the bill Juanita gave me. Just in time, just before I wad it into a ball and drop-kick it onto the street, I realize it has way too much writing on it for just the price of coffee. Uncrumpling it, I smooth it out to discover it says:

4 P.M. 7-11 BEHIND SHELL STN.

There isn't enough time to drive the twenty-two miles to Lavner Bay and back again, so I kill an hour by driving around Nautilus twice. And I still have time to spare. So three-fifty finds me parked at

the end of the street that runs behind the Shell
station. Bored, anxious, and about suffocating from
exhaust fumes, I sit here watching innumerable cars,
whole fleets of trucks, and herds of land behemoths
navigate their way under the bright yellow canopy to
be refueled. This whole gas station business is
decidedly phallic. I mean, think about it for cripe's
sake: attracted by the red, yellow or green of the gas
company corporate logo, vehicles pull into stations all
over the country, their very presence at the pumps
signifying receptivity. Then, behold! A servant of
OPEC, a Petroleum Avatar approaches — a uniformed
youth who (at least in Oregon, anyhow) is the only
one who can handle the sacred organ of transmission,
the Great Gas Nozzle. Gasp! Watch how he
reverently removes the shiny chrome probe from its
socket, observe how he carefully locates the waiting
vehicle's orifice, and before you can say petrodollar,
behold, how he makes the two one! God, only a man
could think up a ritual like this.

"So whaddya want to know about Alyce?" says a
voice from behind me.

I turn, embarrassed that my flight of fancy has
made me neglect my PI duties. It's Juanita, sporting
loud floral mid-calf tights, an oversized white T-shirt,
sunglasses, and a Big Gulp. She leans against my car,
watching the parade of cars into the Shell station.

"I'm in the wrong business," she says. "I shoulda
opened a gas station instead of a coffee shop."

"So you own your own business?" I ask,
wondering if I should tell her that The Grile is
misspelled.

"Yeah, it's mine," she says proudly. "And you
might not think so, but I do a pretty good trade in

the mornings when the by-the-month working stiffs from the cabins are trying to get their eyes open. And the fishermen are always in a hurry to get to their boats. Coffee, toast, hash browns, and two eggs for two forty-nine. I only serve breakfasts and I serve a lot of them. None of those ex-pressos or latties." She laughs. "My customers wouldn't know what to do with them. Me neither for that matter."

I decide to come right to the point. "Alyce's kid, Minou — she's staying with a friend of mine. And the friend is, um, well she doesn't know much about kids. So she's wondering about Minou's father..." I trail off, hoping Juanita will rise to the bait.

"So the kid's safe?" she asks off-handedly and I realize that she's a lot happier about this than she's letting on.

"Yeah. She's safe."

She takes a hefty slurp of her Big Gulp. "So what's your friend wondering?"

Oh brother, make it hard, lady. "She's wondering what kind of a father he is. If he treated the kid okay. That kind of thing."

"Oh she's wondering that, is she?" Juanita says. "And what makes her think I'd know anything about it?"

"Because you were Alyce's friend," I say, realizing I'm only guessing. But it feels right.

"Yeah, maybe I was," she says sadly. "But I couldn't stop her from being stupid, could I? No, I couldn't do that. Alyce and me, we talked about... well, we talked about lots of things. I even told her I'd give her the money to go home."

Now, this really shocks me. "You did?" I ask. "Then why the hell did she hang around?"

Juanita finishes her Big Gulp and walks across the street to put it in a trash can. For a moment I think she's going to keep on walking, but no, she comes back and leans against the car again, arms crossed. "There's a certain kind of woman can't live without a man. It's like there's a big piece of them missing," she says disgustedly. "And nothin' they do for themselves or nothin' they get or nothin' they become is ever enough. Do y'know what I mean?"

"I think so," I tell her. Not from personal experience of course, but I had plenty of straight friends who fit that description. Juanita's a pretty astute lady and my estimation of her rises several notches. "So what you're telling me is that Alyce couldn't leave her husband, not even when you offered to send her back home."

She nods. "He's a shit, that one. Name's Remy. Skinny little Cajun, all charm and Frenchie words. But he never fooled me a bit. He's a user. White trash."

"A user — is he a druggie?" I ask.

She shakes her head. "No. Gamblin's his problem. Drinkin', too. I mean that he uses people. Women. But Alyce couldn't see that."

I decide to play my trump card. "Minou, the kid, said that he owes a gambling debt to some guys from Los Angeles. She says that to pay it off, her father . . . gave her to them."

She comes off the car as though she's been hit with a cattle prod. "Damn! So that's why she ran away. After the police left I gave Remy the note and the money and he took Minou back to the cabin. I thought he was going to do what Alyce asked — to buy a bus ticket and send the kid home. But I guess he had better uses for the money."

So that was what was in the envelope the kid told me about — instructions about what to do with her. "But why would Alyce trust him with money?" I have to ask. "I mean, he'd just ripped off her paycheck."

"Ripped off her —"

"Paycheck, yeah. That's why she went out and stole that digital camera or whatever it was. To pay the rent on the cabin. And to send the kid home."

"Ah, hell," is all Juanita can think of to say.

"That's why I'd have thought that Alyce would have asked you to take care of sending the kid home."

Juanita looks acutely embarrassed. "We'd had . . . words, Alyce and me. Over Remy."

"You mean an argument?"

"Yeah. The day before she got arrested. It was a doozie, too. We said things couldn't never be taken back. Things were so bad we couldn't work together. I told her she'd need to be findin' herself another job." Juanita sighs. "Anyhow, the kid's alright, stayin' with this friend of yours?"

I nod.

Juanita chews vigorously, clearly masticating some problem along with her gum. "Listen, I gotta tell you this. Remy, well, he's a little off."

"Off?"

She makes a circle beside her temple with one finger. "Nuts. Cuckoo. He's a few fries short of a Happy Meal, y'know?"

I sigh. "Okay."

She ticks off items on her fingers. "He's nuts, mean, broke, and in trouble with guys who he owes money to. If he gets his hands on the kid, he'll do whatever he has to do to weasel out of it. So I sure hope your friend hid her good. And I hope she's not even considerin' givin' her back."

I shake my head. "No. She won't give the kid back. And there's no way in the world he could know where she is."

"Are you sure? Are you absolutely sure? Because if there's even a teeny-tiny way, he'll find it. And he'll come and get her."

I'm beginning to feel a little spooked here and contemplate the traffic pulling into the Shell station as if Remy himself might be at the wheel of one of the cars. And he might, I realize, thinking that I wouldn't recognize him if he came walking up the steps of the B & B and asked for a room.

"Does he drive?"

Juanita shrugs. "Doesn't everyone?"

"What I mean is, does he have a car?"

She chews rhythmically, thinking about this. "Nah. He'd of sold it if he had one. Or maybe not. Men and their cars are hard to separate."

"Well, what does he look like?"

"Ugly. He's a scrawny little thing, hardly any

bigger than a football team's water boy. Greasy black hair and dark eyes, pasty-lookin' skin. And he's jittery, y'know?"

This creature sounds so unappetizing that I can't help my observation. "What in hell would any self-respecting woman see in a jerk like that?"

She laughs. "Well now, that's the big question, isn't it?" Sighing, she stands up straight, massaging the area above her kidneys. "I'm going home to sit in the Jacuzzi. Being a business owner is hell on the back. If you need me, I'll be at the coffee shop or at home. I'm in the book. Last name's Crab. Just like it sounds. Good luck to 'ya. And to the kid, too."

"Juanita," I call, and she turns back to me wearily. "Minou thinks her mom is getting out of jail next week. Did you, I mean —"

"Did I tell her that? Hell, no. I haven't talked to Alyce since the day the cops took her away. Or Minou, either."

"I wonder where she got that idea, then."

Juanita shrugs. "She's a smart kid. She would of figured out how to get someone to phone for her and find out. I got the impression from Alyce that this isn't the first trouble she's been in, so the kid might know the drill."

Just before she takes off down the sidewalk, she turns. "What is your friend going to do with her. The kid?"

I shrug. "We, she I mean, doesn't know. Probably Child Protective Services. My friend is trying to find her family back in Louisiana. With that information, CPS could maybe send her back to them."

"That could work," she says. "That's what her

mother wanted." Then, with a rueful smile, she says, "Lavner Bay. That oughta be far enough away."

I'm shocked. How the hell does she know that I'm from Lavner Bay. Then I remember — I'm driving the B & B's car, the one with the sign on it. Boy, talk about stupid. Far enough away? I sure hope so.

Chapter 11

"Just in time!" Ossie calls as I come up the steps of the B & B.

"Time for what?" I ask, tired, hungry, and more than a little crabby.

"Time for us to leave. Kerry's going to take me to get pictures of Swimming Cat Cove."

Then I remember. "For the Web page," I say. "Okay. Where's Kerry?"

"Here," Kerry says, coming down the stairs looking harried, zipping her anorak and handing her camera bag to Ossie. "Get that tripod, will you," she calls to Minou and the kid jumps to help her.

"Any luck?" I ask.

"Too much luck," she says, looking worried. "There must be five hundred Trudeaus in that burg. I'll tell you all about it when I get back. Oh, and I moved my stuff in with yours. We had a couple of folks from Portland who wanted a room and I thought you probably wanted the income more than you wanted privacy. And I don't snore," she adds, grinning. "Gotta go. The magic light."

"The what?"

"The magic light. Late afternoon or early morning light is best for photographs. Makes them look —"

"Magic. I'll whip up something for supper."

Knowing my culinary skills, Kerry looks alarmed. It's not a joke that I only tackle dishes which have no more than four ingredients and fit into one pan. Casserole is my middle name. "Not that tuna thing again with the noodles and the mushroom soup?"

"Maybe," I say. "At least Ossie will eat it."

"Yeah, it does have that virtue," she agrees.

"Are you related to Martha Stewart?" I ask her, only half-kidding.

"Martha who?"

"PI'ing, computers, photography, cooking. Heck, you're even good with kids. You're the woman who can do everything. You'll make someone a terrific wife, Owyhee," I tell her grumpily.

She gives me a very strange look indeed and as she closes the front door behind her, it occurs to me that maybe I've offended her and I want to call her back, but I'm suddenly smitten with awkwardness.

Because maybe she thinks I mean that a fitting role for her would be to be some guy's, you know, wife, and I've never even heard her mention a man. Or maybe she thinks I mean that a fitting role for her would be to be some chick's wife, and I've never heard her mention a woman. And what about the Martha Stewart comment? Oh God, I've probably committed about six errors of political correctness. Hell. I plunk my rear end down on the stool behind the reception desk and watch Kerry's truck spit gravel.

"Shit," I mutter under my breath.

"Rarrrr," Sammy agrees, coming to sit on the desk where he thinks I might be working.

"Don't fart, okay?" I warn him. "I'm in no mood to put up with a flatulent cat." He gives me a wounded look. "So is she or isn't she?" I ask him. "If I knew, I could stop getting in trouble making stupid jokes. Jeez, between the Indian thing and the sexual preference thing, I sometimes feel like I'm walking through a minefield with Kerry."

Sammy rumbles his agreement and I hunt around for the NO VACANCY sign.

"C'mon, let's go put this out," I tell him. "You can get rid of your gas outside." He joins me as we walk through the little garden with the koi pond along a path to the highway. There I affix the NO VACANCY sign to the larger (and quite expensive) blue and white job I had constructed last year advertising the presence of LAVNER BAY BED AND BREAKFAST in large letters for the passing throng. Aunt Grace may have wanted to keep the B & B a secret; I can't afford to. Taking a certain amount of satisfaction in the fact that hey, we're full, I call

Sammy and we meander back through the garden. Garden, ha. The flowerbeds are overrun with weeds and all the annuals need re-planting. I'll have to hunt down my aunt's gardener, I realize, and try to remember the name of the not-so-young but disgustingly healthy and in-terrific-shape woman Kaye pointed out to me at The Daily Grind one morning. A marathon runner, I think Kaye said she was. Thin. Good biceps. Hmmm, what was her name — Sandy, Cindy, Callie, something like that. Well, Kaye would certainly remember.

I sit for a minute more on the bench, wondering why this part of the coast attracts more than its share of older, capable, free-spirited, damn-it-to-hell, throw-away-their-bras, flannel-and-Birkenstock lesbians. And marveling at the fact that they all seem to know one another. How do they do it? Do they all have tricorders like the crew members on *Star Trek,* tricorders that glow lavender whenever a newcomer approaches a local lesbian? I'm definitely missing out on something and feel a pang of genuine longing. How does one infiltrate the "in" group anyhow? And then it strikes me — maybe all I have to do is take the first step. I mean, it's not as though I don't know where to start. I mean, there's Robin, and Kaye, and . . . Suddenly the hair rises a little on the back of my neck. Because right there by the koi pond, right there where a careless or in-a-hurry someone would have thrown it, is a half-smoked cigarette. I walk over to pick it up, knowing before I do what I'll find — an unfiltered Camel.

Suddenly my quaint, shady garden seems full of menace. "Hey, Sammy, c'mon," I call, not wanting him out here prowling around in the bushes.

"Supper." Hearing the magic word, he comes running. And all the way back to the B & B, I imagine I can feel eyes boring into my back. Because the cigarette, which I'm holding between my finger and thumb, is still smoldering.

So I'm sitting at the registration desk, cigarette stubbed out and safely stowed in a plastic baggie, wondering what in hell to do with this odious *thing* when I hear Kerry's truck pull up. Great. Just great. Have I made supper? Hell, have I even fed Sammy as I promised I would? No. I've just sat here fretting. I bury the bagged butt under some paperwork and hie myself off to the kitchen, where they find me tossing celery, onions, mushrooms, and green pepper into the sink and filling a pot with water. Those ingredients, combined with a can of mushroom soup, some noodles, and a tin of tuna, comprise the "tuna thing" that Kerry spoke of so disparagingly. And okay, yes, it does stretch my abilities, consisting as it does of more than four ingredients, but cooks need to challenge themselves now and then, right? And considering the recipe (learned from a college roommate) originally consisted of a bag of frozen veggies instead of the oh-so-healthful fresh ones I use, I feel I'm being positively reckless.

"Oh, the tuna thing," Ossie says neutrally, depositing Kerry's tripod in the corner.

I'm surprised. "What? Not 'oh no, the tuna thing?' "

"Kerry said I needed to eat fish," Ossie reminds me, tucking her blonde hair back behind her ears in a gesture clearly copied from Kerry. "I like your tuna thing and I just realized that even though it comes in a can, tuna *is* fish."

"Kerry's right," I tell her. "You need to eat more veggies fast. Your brain's rotting."

"Ha, ha," she says, but I hear a note of worry in her voice.

"So did you get your pictures?" I ask, brandishing a chopping knife. Ossie, I note, stands well back.

"We got terrific pictures!" Kerry says, coming through the back door with Minou trailing her, camera bag in hand. "Right, kids?"

"Right!" they chorus.

"The cove is terrific!" Ossie tells me, plunking herself down at the table. "We could even see the cave where I think the cat took shelter. It's not always above water, but the tide was going out so we could see it plain as day."

"And up top, on the grass, we found a hole," Minou adds excitedly. "Kerry thinks something lives in it and that it maybe connects to the cave."

"Oh yeah?" I say, not really paying attention to all this cat cave nonsense. Kerry picks up on my lack of enthusiasm.

"Kids, why don't you go wash up for supper. Half an hour. You can check out the programs we loaded on your computer, Ossie."

Ossie looks at me quizzically, but does as she's asked.

"What's up?" Kerry asks, once the girls have thundered upstairs.

"Go look on the reception desk, under the VISA slips," I tell her. "There's a plastic baggie. Bring it on in here."

She's back in a flash, turning the baggie over in her hands, peering at it closely. "The smoker again," she says. "Where did you find this?"

"In the garden. Right beside the koi pond. I'd gone outside to put the NO VACANCY sign up."

"Damn. No way to know when it was left."

"Oh yes there is. It was still burning when I noticed it."

"Shit," Kerry says. "Who was on the premises besides you?"

"No one," I tell her. "I checked the parking lot. Everyone's car was gone."

"*Bloody* hell," she says. "I was hoping it'd turn out to be one of the guests."

"Me, too. Because if it isn't one of the guests..." I shrug.

"Then it's someone hanging around," she supplies.

"Kerry, I thought this all through last night and I'd just about decided that one of the guests was responsible. But I got up too late to ask questions. Everyone had gone off to brunch or trot through the tidepools or whatever tourists do on a nice Sunday at the beach."

She runs a hand though her hair. "Let's find out," she says.

"Find out?"

"Yeah, find out. What — aren't I speaking English? I know you looked in the parking lot, but until you've asked everyone, we can't be sure. After all, just because a car was gone doesn't mean that both passengers were gone, too. All it really means is that the driver was gone. Right?"

"Right," I say, because I know that's what she wants me to say.

"I've heard people coming in," she says. "I'm going to start asking some questions if that's okay with you. And while I'm gone, please go ahead and chop. I'm starving. Even for your tuna thing."

So she leaves me preparing the meal, trying not to add one of my digits to the casserole. I dice and mince, venting my anxiety and frustration on innocent vegetables, trying not to be depressed, because who in her right mind smokes anyhow, let alone unfiltered Camels? This seems like a man thing to me, and that makes me even more anxious. Consequently, by the time I have the casserole assembled and in the oven, I'm more than a trifle jumpy and when Ossie appears in the kitchen door, I let out a pretty good yell.

"What?" I holler, trying to cover my distress.

She hangs back diffidently, Sammy in her arms. "I saw him," she says.

"Saw him? Who him?"

"The guy Kerry's asking everyone about. The guy who was smoking."

"You did?"

She looks over her shoulder and I realize she's looking for Minou. "Yesterday just before supper," Ossie says, lowering her voice. "I went out to feed the fish. He didn't think I saw him, but I did."

"Ossie. My God, why didn't you tell someone?"

She shrugs. "I was going to, but when I checked it out later, you know, just to be sure, he was gone. So I didn't want to be like the kid who cried wolf, you know. And when I went out just now to feed the koi, he wasn't there either. So there's nothing to tell."

"What, um, did you see what he looked like?"

Ossie knows now that something's up and her kid's brain zaps ahead at warp speed to the conclusion that my creaky old impulse engines are chugging toward — a conclusion I don't want to reach. "It's Minou's father, isn't it?" she asks, not at all astonished. Because after all, she wants to believe in the things that Agent Mulder of *The X-Files* wants to believes in — alien abductions, spontaneous human combustion, crop circles, speaking in tongues. Nothing is too unlikely for Ossie and Mulder. "It's him. He's come to try and take her away."

"How could it be him?" I ask hoarsely and ungrammatically. "There's no way in the world he could know where she is." When Ossie says nothing, I ask her, my eleven-year-old Delphic oracle: "Well, is there?"

Ossie looks away, shaking her head, and I realize that she's probably searching her database of the paranormal for the answer to this problem. I'm worried now, because what if she insists that aliens told him or some such claptrap? But to my relief, she says nothing.

"Okay, let's be calm here," I say, feeling far from calm, sitting down hard. "Where is she? Minou?"

"Upstairs playing a video game." Ossie looks at me out of her ancient eyes. "Sim City 2000."

"Go get her," I say. "And tell Kerry to come down here, too. Don't . . . say anything to Minou about this, okay?"

"Okay," Ossie says, solemn. She hesitates in the doorway. "I know you're angry, but you're not going to, you know, let her father have her, are you?"

"The way I feel right now I'd let Attilla the Hun have her if it brought me peace and quiet! Go!"

When she's gone, I pace around the kitchen, only barely restraining myself from tearing my hair out, literally, great handfuls of it. This situation has turned out to be (as I predicted) one humungous mess. What Ossie has suggested is impossible — there's no way Minou's father could know where she is. Well, is there?

"Allison," Kerry says quietly from behind me. "I told the kids to stay in Ossie's room."

I'm pissed until I see her face — grim and serious like maybe someone died. "Hey — what's going on?"

"C'mon, let's go to the reception desk. Unless I'm wrong and the guy lurking on the front porch is really trying to read your electric meter, I think we're about to meet Minou's father."

So even though my throat's too dry to swallow, I feel okay because I'll just follow Kerry's lead. I mean, she must have handled hundreds of situations like this — well, dozens, anyhow. Evidently I'm transmitting this to her telepathically, because she gives me a flat, hard-eyed look and I can tell that she's psyching herself up. The front door tinkles closed and we move together, Tweedledum and Tweedledee, closing ranks against the enemy. Oh goody.

"Can we help you?" I inquire brightly as a skinny man dressed in dirty jeans and a green plaid jacket sidles in. He takes a quick look around, pats his slicked-back hair, gives me the benefit of a smile that could use considerable dental work, and hitches up his pants. I continue, "We're full, but the motel across the way —"

"You can cut the crap," he says conversationally, going over to look up the big, broad staircase to the second floor. "You know what I want."

"Call the cops," Kerry tells me, giving me a little push toward the reception desk. I find I'm eager to oblige, and I dial 911 in a flash. "Mister, I don't know what you want, but we've already told you that we have no rooms. So you might as well go," Kerry says in a far-from-friendly voice. This new, kick-ass Kerry is a Kerry I've never seen and I'm impressed. Heck, I'd go if she talked to me like that.

However, the creature is not impressed. Looking her up and down, he does what so many men have done for centuries to women — he underestimates her.

"I'm gonna get my kid," he sneers, taking a step toward her, trying to intimidate her with his fearsome five-foot-seven presence. "Are you gonna stop me?"

When he gets close enough, Kerry sighs, and quicker than you can say spit, jams several fingers into his face. In amazement, I see she has hooked his nose.

"Oh, *bon Dieu*," he cries, falling to his knees, flapping his arms like a goose.

"Hands on your head," Kerry says conversationally. "Oh, no, no, no — don't touch your nose or I'll be forced to rip it off."

I'm totally, like, flabberasted, because I've never seen this nose thing or even read about it. Well there is the movie *Chinatown*, but in it Jack Nicholson got

104

his nose *sliced*. What Kerry's doing to this little weasel is more in the way of mangling him. Even Sammy's astounded, pausing in the midst of cleaning his balls to follow the proceedings.

"Sshh," Kerry says. "Be quiet now. And listen." The creature listens, tears and snot running out of his nose, nodding frantically. I hear the siren of the Lavner Bay cop car turning off the highway onto our driveway but I can't take my eyes off Kerry. "We don't have your kid. You're mistaken. I'm going to take my fingers out of your nose and when the cop comes in, you can tell him whatever you want. But you're going to stay away from here. Okay?"

"*Oui, oui,* yeah, sure," he gabbles, rising to his feet as soon as Kerry lets go of him. I'm relieved to see that she takes one step back, just in case Remy is a sore (ha, ha) loser.

The heavy footsteps of one of Lavner Bay's two cops sound on the B & B's steps and I gird my loins for the necessary lies.

"Well, well," the florid, pain-in-the-butt deputy says, his large blue-shirted masculine presence filling the lobby like a cloud of bad karma. "You ladies having some trouble here?"

Hell, no, we called you for fun. "This, ah, gentleman became unruly and refused to leave the premises when we told him we had no rooms available," I say indignantly.

Deputy Johanssen, as close to being a reptile as evolution will allow, blinks pale eyes and thinks this over. "That's a four-thirty-six. A misdemeanor," he says sternly, looking me up and down as if I, and not the creature here, had committed the offense. I know what he's thinking: why drag him out of his nice warm office for something so petty? Couldn't we women handle this? Instead, I assume a worried, damsel-like demeanor and cast worried eyes upon Minou's father who is surreptitiously wiping his nose on his sleeve.

"He, this gentleman, became quite offensive. He frightened us. I was afraid he might frighten my guests. Could you just take him away? I don't want to press charges or anything like that. I know you're a busy man."

Clearly relieved that he's not going to have to do any tedious paperwork, Johanssen agrees. "Hmmmf," he responds finally, hitching up *his* pants. God, why do men do that? Are they afraid that something's fallen off since last they hitched? "C'mon, you," he says to the creature, peering at him closely. "That nose looks bad. Got a cold, have you? Why don't you go find yourself a room in a motel and don't cause these nice ladies no more trouble, hear?"

Remy nods, giving Kerry a look that says they have unfinished business. I groan. How did I know that the nose thing wouldn't do it?

"Go get in the cruiser," Johanssen says gruffly, holding the door for Remy as he slouches down the steps. "I'll just give you a ride to the next town." He tips his hat to us, an ambiguous smile on his face. "Miz O'Neil. Miz Owyhee. Y'all have a nice day now."

"Up yours," Kerry says as the door swings shut behind him.

I'm puzzled. "What's the problem? At least he took him away."

"Johanssen is the biggest misanthropist in the world," she says. "And right after women come Indians. In fact, maybe the only living thing he can stand is himself. Why haven't you Lavner Bayites voted him and that cretin of a sheriff out of office, anyhow? Hell, Sammy would do a better job."

"Sammy can't drive," I remind her. "Say, where did you learn to do that nose thing?"

She actually looks embarrassed. "Oh, that. From my cousin Daniel. It's a great thing to use on schoolyard bullies. There's a throat thing that's good too, but my hand isn't strong enough."

Still feeling dazed, I follow her into the kitchen where she's using a nail brush and lots of hot water and soap on her hands, muttering under her breath. "What is it?" I ask her. "Remy or Johanssen?"

She shakes her head, still angry, still scrubbing. "Let's get the kids," she says. "This shouldn't have happened. That guy shouldn't have been able to trace Minou. I want to know how he did. And I've got a feeling they can tell us. Or one of them, anyhow."

I'm agog. "What? You think one of them told him? Who — Minou?"

"Well, Ossie wouldn't, now would she?" she says, drying her hands, "So who does that leave?"

"But why? Minou's afraid of him. Isn't she?"

"Let's find out. I'll go get them."

I sit down heavily at the table, this new thought buzzing around in my brain like a gnat. Sensing my distress, Sammy has come to rub companionably against my leg, and I pat him absently, still upset, not caring if he farts a blue cloud.

I hear her coming into the kitchen before I see her. "Shit!" she says, holding up a note that she's torn off Ossie's printer.

I CAN'T LET YOU GIVE MINOU BACK TO HER FATHER. I'VE TAKEN HER SOMEPLACE WHERE SHE'LL BE SAFE UNTIL HER MOTHER GETS OUT OF JAIL ON TUESDAY. PLEASE DON'T BE TOO MAD.

OSSIE

Chapter 12

"Terrific," I tell Kerry as we sit semi-stunned at the kitchen table. "Just terrific. And it's even more terrific because it's my fault."

"Your fault? Why your fault?"

"Because I was mad at Ossie, dammit. When she told me that she'd seen some guy hanging around the koi garden and hadn't told me, I said I might let Attilla the Hun have Minou if it would bring peace and quiet to this place."

"Ohhh," Kerry groans.

"Yeah. I know. Stupid."

"Okay, let's not beat ourselves up over this, let's just try to figure out what to do. Where would Ossie have taken Minou? If she doesn't consider this place safe — and it evidently isn't because Remy found it, what would she consider safe? Someplace out of town? A relative's?"

I shake my head. "Pan and Ossie don't have any relatives around here. According to Pan, when she found out her husband had left with the boys, she was so pissed off that she packed Ossie into the car and they just started driving west. They only stopped along the way to eat. And they slept in the car, too. Then, when they reached Lavner Bay, the car broke down. That's how they ended up here. That was three years ago." I put my head in my hands and try to think about who Ossie's friends are. And come up empty. Because I can't concentrate. All I can think about is what Pan is going to say if anything happens to Ossie. And how I'm going to feel — worse than I do already. Much worse. "I —" I shake my head, as if to dislodge an answer.

"Okay, let's take a break," Kerry says, reaching over and squeezing my shoulder. "They're gone. But from what you've told me, I don't think Ossie will go too far. She's not running away, she's helping Minou, right? Keeping her safe."

I nod.

"So she'll want to stick around someplace close by until Tuesday — the day she thinks Alyce is getting out of jail. All we have to do is figure out where that place is. So let's have dinner and think. Isn't that tuna thing of yours about done?"

I burst into tears. "That sounds so fucking British!"

"Excuse me?" Kerry says, alarmed by my outburst.

"That sounds so fucking British — you know, they always have tea in a crisis. As if eating or drinking could defuse the situation."

She hands me a paper towel and I wipe my face, blowing my nose, which makes me think of Remy's nose so I start laughing but pretty soon the gravity of the situation kind of digs its claws into me and before I know it, I'm bawling again. "Here," Kerry says, shoving a glass of wine under my nose. "It's not tea, but it's another one of the white man's cures for everything — firewater."

I drink dutifully. "Waste of good pinot noir," I tell her. "But pour me another glass, will you?" As she does so, I bring her up to date on my visit to Nautilus and Juanita.

"Think Ossie might've taken Minou there?" Kerry asks.

"I don't know. I guess we ought to check, though." Then a thought occurs to me. "Aren't we going to have to tell the sheriff about all this? About Remy losing Minou in the card game? About the LA movie producers?"

Kerry considers this. "Yeah. We have to. Just for the record, if nothing else. That way, if anything goes wrong, it'll be their asses and not ours."

I'm alarmed all over again. "What do you think might go wrong?"

"Nothing," she says soothingly. "I think we'll probably find the kids ourselves. Reporting them missing won't do a damned bit of good because I don't think that pair of clowns will take us seriously." She snorts. "And even if they do, how valuable an asset do you think Johanssen would be in a search?"

"An asshole is more like it," I mutter.

She smiles. "Yeah, he is, isn't he. But he and Sheriff Belcher are The Law in these here parts, ma'am, and if by some chance we don't find the kids we're going to want to have them involved. They're hooked up with all those missing kids databases."

I feel faint just thinking about it. "Pan really will kill me," I predict.

"It won't happen," Kerry says confidently. "We're going to find them. We do have one small problem, though."

"And that is?"

"We're not going to be the only ones looking for the kids."

"Oh yeah," I say. "Him."

"Yeah. Him. Somehow I don't think he's going quietly back to Nautilus with his tail between his legs. I think he'll be hanging around somewhere close by, watching and waiting."

"Now there's something useful Belcher and Johanssen could do," I suggest. "Pick Remy up. Remove him from the equation."

Kerry snorts again. "On our word alone? Hell, not even on our word — on the word of a runaway kid?"

"Nuts."

"I'm working on getting Remy's rap sheet," Kerry says. "I'm sure the guy has one. When I get it, that ought to influence Belcher and Johanssen. They might just pick Remy up then."

"So when should we go to the cops?" I ask, looking forward to the coming interview about as much as a visit to the periodontist.

112

"How about now? The office will still be open. Barely. So let's get it over with — it's just a formality, right?"

"Right," I agree, hoping that she's right, too, about our being the ones likely to find them. Because the alternative really is unthinkable.

A visit to the periodontist would have been preferable. We supplied the necessary information while Johanssen filled in a seemingly interminable series of forms, glancing disapprovingly or disbelievingly at us every chance he got. The whole ordeal took at least an hour and a half and when it was done, I had the feeling that we'd better try our hardest to find the kids. Johanssen's heart just wasn't in this, especially once I told him that Ossie had run away — well, not really run away, but had just taken off — twice before.

"So what's the next step?" I make the mistake of asking him once he's put the forms in a folder and is ushering us out the door.

"You let us handle things, now," he replies. "We're the professionals. We know what to do, ma'am. You should have told me all this before," he chides. "When I came out on that four-thirty-six. Could've saved us a lot of grief."

I grind my teeth together in frustration. "Maybe," I say. "But what are you going to *do*?" I want to know. "Are you going to pick up Remy LaPlante? Start looking for the kids?"

"I'm going to talk this over with Sheriff Belcher and if he thinks we ought to, why we'll start the

113

wheels in motion," he says soothingly, having maneuvered us onto the porch where he closes the door behind us.

"What wheels?" I ask the closed door, barely restraining myself from kicking it. "The ones on the truck that's going to take you to the Salty Dawg Saloon to guzzle a vat of beer when you get off work?"

"C'mon," Kerry says. "We knew he wouldn't take us seriously. So now we know we're on our own. Let's go have supper then get to work."

"Not bad," Kerry says, holding up a forkful of my tuna casserole. "Not bad at all," and I feel absurdly like Ossie for a moment — grateful for the approval of Kerry the Capable, the Coast's Queen of Competence, mistress of every situation from nanobytes to noses. And then I feel guilty because she's giving me a compliment after all and why am I having such a problem being gracious? Interesting.

By the time we've finished dessert — half a gallon of Espresso Madness ice cream — we have a list of places we need to check. All within 24 hours. Sensing my incipient hysteria, Kerry tries to soothe me.

"A lot of these we can check by phone — I'll go use my car phone. You stay and use the phone here." But when the door closes behind her, it seems awfully lonely in the B & B. Oh, sure a lot of the guests have returned from their evening's frolics, but it still seems lonely. And, as much as I hate to admit it, I'm more than a little scared. What if we don't find Minou before her father finds her? What if Ossie gets hurt in the process? What if Remy nabs both of them? To silence the clamoring in my mind I pick up the phone and start dialing.

Fifteen minutes later, I have ascertained that Ossie isn't at her friend Erica's; at Few Mornings — where she sometimes picked up a couple of bucks clearing tables and washing dishes; at Frog Hollow where, until now, she had used Jameson's Internet access; at the ice cream place in Windsock; at the fish deli in Lavner Bay where she hung out and listened to the tall tales of the aged and slightly addled proprietor (he was the one who had first told her about Swimming Cat Cove); or at the skateboard park. Hanging up the phone, I grind my teeth in frustration because that leaves the rest of the list — the local places that have to be checked in person tomorrow because they're closed now. And another list of Unsavory Places. Like the boarded-up bathroom at the state park. Or the junked car out on Top o'the Hill Drive. And the alley behind the Safeway store in Nautilus — Minou's former home. Feeling discouraged, I put my head in my hands and briefly consider weeping.

"Is this a good time?" a cheerful voice asks.

I look up and it's Eve. Of course it's Eve, the irrepressible, ever-smiling, people-liking, capital-possessing, B & B-coveting Eve, Eve who I'd like to, right at the moment, kill.

"Actually, it's not," I tell her, praying for forbearance. "It's one of the worst times I can remember."

"Oh," she says, her smile dimming from a hundred and fifty watts to a hundred. "What's wrong?"

I see no harm in telling her. Half of the truth anyhow. "The kid who helps around here — you may have noticed her, little blonde-haired kid, smart as can be — well, she's kinda disappeared."

"Oh, no!" she gasps.

"Oh yes."

"Did someone, I mean, do you suspect —"

I shake my head. "No. She left a note. She's just gone until Tuesday. She thinks she's helping another kid out. But I want to find her."

"Of course, absolutely," Eve says. "Listen, Katherine checked out. I mean literally. She's gone back to Tucson. So I could help — you know, look after things here while you look for the child. If you like."

I know I'm giving her the strangest look. Actually, that's exactly what I'd like. Kerry will presumably be back any minute and then we can go together to check the bathrooms, back alleys, and junked cars of the Central Coast. It's not that I'm a wimp, it's just that well, darn it, I'm not particularly brave. And after the nose episode, I'm convinced that Kerry is. So maybe I can keep her company in her truck and, like, entertain her, while we drive from unsavory location to unsavory location. So what does that make me — a PI's moll?

"Ha!" I say in response to my musings, and Eve takes a step back. "Sorry," I tell her. "I was thinking about something else. Yes, I'd love it if you took care of things here while I looked for her. Ossie. Her name is Ossie. She's blonde, eleven, and . . ." My stomach clenches at the next word, because it's *gone*. *Blonde, eleven, and gone.*

Eve nods, impressed by the responsibility I'm giving her. "Okay. Show me what to do."

"Basically, just hang out here and tell folks that

we don't have any rooms," I tell her. "If people want to check out, find their ticket and calculate the charge. If they want, you know, more towels, or tea, or the TV Guide, or whatever, just tell them to look around on the third floor. At nine o'clock, lock the front and back doors. And make sure the cat is in."

"When will you be back?"

"God knows," I say, hearing the crunch of tires on the front driveway. A quick look out the window confirms the presence of Kerry's truck and I grab my jacket and hurry outside to meet her. "Thanks," I call to Eve. The last I see of her she's still smiling.

By ten o'clock, Kerry and I are tired, frustrated, and although we're only halfway through our list of unsavory places, I've seen enough of them to last me forever.

"How do you know about all these places?" I ask her as we turn our flashlights on the interior of the Yoko Beach ladies' loo.

"Runaways," she says. "PIs look for a lot of runaways. In the big cities we tail philandering spouses. Here we try to find missing kids and young women."

"That's pretty sad," I say. "Do you find them?"

She turns off her light and we walk together out into the moonlight. A dark ribbon of water — Badger Creek — winds through the park grounds to the sea, and off to our right the waves hiss against the sandy shore. "Sometimes. Too often, they're dead, though."

I shiver. "You're scaring me. What happens?"

She taps her mag light against her leg. "What

117

happens? Hell, there are a dozen answers. Maybe some young girl does something she doesn't realize is risky, like taking a drive with a neighbor or some guy who hangs around with her brother. Maybe this guy is the first one to ever pay any attention to her. Maybe they drive out into the country and he plays the radio and tells her jokes and she's trusting and relaxed and she really, really likes him and she never wants to go back to dull, boring old Windsock, especially when he tells her why don't they just take off for oh, Las Vegas, and never come back?" Kerry's voice has gotten husky and all of a sudden I'm sorry I asked. "That's one maybe," she says, "and there are probably as many maybes as there are dead bodies. Anyhow, no matter how the kids were lured away, the outcomes are pretty much the same — a body floating in a bog, a shallow grave in the woods, a boarded-up shack with a smell coming out of it that's so bad that you have to stick Vicks up your nose just to get near the place." She laughs bitterly. "Those are some pieces of coastal lore you don't want on your Web site."

I'm shocked into silence because this is a side of Kerry I've never seen. "I didn't know you took jobs like this," I tell her. "They sound . . . awful."

"They are," she says wearily. "I don't do missing kids anymore if I can help it."

"I'm sorry I dragged you into this," I say, feeling terrible.

She shrugs. "Don't be sorry. I'm glad I was around so I could help. But let's knock things off for tonight," she says brusquely and I realize she doesn't want to talk about this missing kids-in-the-bog thing anymore. Who could blame her? Neither do I. "We'll split up again tomorrow and I'll do the back alleys and the rest of the state parks. You can do Ossie's in-town hangouts in person. We'll find the kids."

Whereas I was a tiny bit hopeful when we set out, I'm wallowing hip-deep in despair now. What Kerry said about the boarded-up shack and the Vicks really got to me. Surely Ossie wouldn't be so stupid as to trust the wrong person?

"Don't give in to it," Kerry advises as we drive through Windsock, the cheery yellow lights of restaurants and motels blazing like beacons against the demons of the dark.

"How do you know what I'm thinking?" I ask as we climb the little hill beside the bay.

"I know."

Maybe she does know, I think wearily. Maybe it's an Indian thing. Or maybe it's a PI thing. Bodies in bogs. I shudder. "It's my fault, you know," I tell her as we cruise out of Windsock and into Lavner Bay.

"Fault, shmault." She pulls into the parking lot and shuts off the lights. "Let's just get some sleep and try to deal with things tomorrow."

There's a note on the registration desk from Eve.

IT WAS FUN. NO PROBLEMS. HOPE YOU FOUND HER. IF NOT I CAN HELP TOMORROW ON REGISTRATION DESK.

Ha, I think to myself. If you're going to work for me tomorrow, Ms. Cheerful, you'll have beds to change, sheets and towels to wash, rooms to vacuum, and toilets to clean. We'll see how much you enjoy being a hotelier after that.

On the third floor, I pass Ossie's room and even though I know she's not there, I push the door open anyhow. Sammy's asleep on her bed, one paw over his eyes, and he moans a little, chasing something in a feline dream. Ossie's computer is still turned on, and as I sit at her desk wondering how to shut the thing off, the door opens behind me.

"It's me," Kerry says. "I couldn't get to sleep. Thought I'd come down and see if Ossie left us," she shrugs, "I don't know, a clue? Something that would help." She clicks a few keys and sighs. "Nothing. Just that note she created in her word-processing program." She punches a button and the screen goes black. "Allison, you know the kid better than I do. Where would you go if you were Ossie?"

"I don't know. She said she was taking Minou someplace safe. I . . . just don't know."

"Well, let's sleep on it," Kerry says. "Maybe something will occur to one of us."

"You know, something's just occurred to me," I say, my stomach sinking. "Ossie will undoubtedly show up at the jail on Tuesday with Minou. So Remy doesn't have to wander around Lavner Bay or Windsock looking for the kids, does he? He just has to wait until Ossie delivers Minou to the courthouse. That's when he'll try to grab her, don't you think?"

She nods. "Yeah. Alyce's bail hearing's on the court docket. It's public knowledge. He could easily find out."

"Why do you suppose he showed up here, then? He was taking quite a chance."

She yawns again. "He's eager. If he really owes some guys some money, he'll want to pay up as fast as he can."

I think some more about what Kerry said about Alyce's bail hearing being public knowledge because this helps to answer a question that's been bugging me. Maybe this is how Minou knows to show up at the courthouse on Tuesday — she got someone to read her the court docket (or did it herself), asked some questions about bail, and didn't quite understand the answer. A natural mistake for a nine-year-old to make, especially a nine-year-old who wants to go home with her mother. Juanita said she was plenty smart, but she's only a kid. So she could easily have gotten things only half right. I try this out on Kerry, and she shrugs, rubbing her eyes.

"That sounds logical," Kerry says, yawning. "But it doesn't really matter, does it? I guess I have less curiosity than you do. All I can think of are these two kids on the streets or in some back alley or junked car, somewhere on the coast, trying to stay out of Remy's way until Tuesday. I mean, there are a lot of things we don't know, but one thing we can be pretty sure of is that both Minou and Remy are going to show up at the jail on Tuesday."

"And Ossie," I add.

"And Ossie," Kerry agrees grimly. "You know, I was thinking that we could just camp out at the jail and snatch Ossie out of the middle of this when she shows up with Minou, but I think we'd better try really hard to find the kids tomorrow. There's too much potential for things to go wrong. If Minou told the truth about the gambling debt, then Remy's going to be one desperate guy." She shrugs. "For all

121

we know he'll bring the so-called movie producers with him."

I groan. This is too much. "I'm going to bed. Tomorrow has to be a better day."

Kerry turns off the light in Ossie's room and we go together up the stairs. "It has to be a better day," she says. "It's the only one we have left."

Chapter 13

I'm wrong. Tomorrow is not a better day. In fact, tomorrow is a day whose worseness could not have been imagined. It begins well enough — a cheery, well-coiffed, toothbrushed, and crisply-clothed Eve (the denim shirt and black jeans she's wearing are quite nice) meets me at the reception desk at six, yes, six o'clock which is before roosters crow let alone before my eyes are open, and she wisely lets me stagger to the kitchen to make coffee before unleashing her goodwill. Kerry's been up and gone for awhile and I feel the hounds of panic nipping at my heels, so I toast some bread, pile it with peanut butter, and pour a cup of coffee.

"Gotta go in a minute," I tell Eve, who has come to join me in the kitchen. "Thanks for helping out." Sammy twines anxiously around my ankles, reminding me of his presence. "Oh, will you feed the cat? I've left a list of things you ought to do. It's on the counter over there. You can wait until check-out to start cleaning the rooms. I usually do."

She nods, serious but still cheerful. "I thought you'd have some real chores for me today."

"Well, you were right."

"No luck?" she asks, clearly not certain to what extent I want to talk about last night.

I shake my head. "No luck. But I'm sure we'll find her today. Kerry thinks so."

Eve nods, a small secretive smile on her lips. "Kerry seems a . . . competent person."

For some reason the smile irritates me. It's almost, well, a smirk. And Kerry is no one to be smirked about. "Competent? Yeah, I guess that's a good word for her."

Eve's smile only gets smirkier.

"She's a PI," I say by way of explanation. "That's why she seems competent. She can do . . . everything."

"Well, that's definite," she says. "So I gather you two are . . ." She lets the question hang.

I'm not sure what she's talking about for a moment but when I get it, I prepare to deliver a pithy retort prefaced by "Ha!" only to find that I've inhaled my toast. Now I'm choking, which forces me to bang my plate down on the table to try and manage my coughing fit. Eve is thumping me on the back, I'm coughing, and finally I'm sitting at the table, tears running down my cheeks, drinking the glass of water she's poured for me.

"Quite an answer," she remarks.

"We're not, you know, a couple," I croak. "And since you asked, I don't think Kerry is even, well . . ."

Eve hoots with laughter. "Of course she is!"

I'm stunned. "She is?"

"Trust me." She peers closely at me. "Where did you say you were from?"

"Lancaster. In the Mojave Desert."

"That explains it," she says. "Your dyke radar's gotten scrambled from living so close to the air force base there."

I take a deep breath and, finding no toast crumbs where they shouldn't be, take my plate and mug to the sink. "My radar may be scrambled," I tell her, "but not that scrambled. Anyhow, I gotta go get dressed now. Thanks again for helping out."

Upstairs, I shower, wash and dry my hair, drag the covers up over my bed and, frantic with the desire to get out of there and start my search, hunt for a pair of clean jeans and a T-shirt. Finding none — I've been moving too fast too settle down and do laundry — I drag a none-too-clean pair of Levis and a questionable white T-shirt out of the closet. I feel bad — Kerry's bed under the gabled window is neatly made and her clothes are hung up just as neatly in the closet. I touch the ironed sleeve of one of her Oxford cloth shirts, remembering Eve's comment about her, then guiltily let the sleeve drop and grab my purple fleece jacket off its hanger, slam the door behind me, and thump down the stairs. There really must be something critically wrong with my radar if it didn't blip on Kerry, I think. Assuming, of course, that Eve is right. At the moment, however, I have more serious things to think about.

As much as I'd like to, I can't exactly go to the local print shop with Ossie's school photo and have a zillion fliers made saying HAVE YOU SEEN ME? First, I don't have time to plaster Lavner Bay and Windsock with them. Second, I do not want to bring to everyone's attention the fact that the kid is missing. Not yet. So that gives us just this one day — a measly 24 hours — to find the kids. And third, I'm still hoping that I can keep this from Pan. So I have to hustle and canvass all Ossie's haunts in person. One by one. Without giving too much away. Great.

As I drive into Windsock, I check the list I made while I was putting on my socks. I know full well that Ossie's two all-time favorite spots are the Aquarium in Nautilus where she can spend endless hours watching the orca they're rehabilitating there, and the top of Cape Aeterna, where she enjoys hanging out in the little stone hut built during World War Two for submarine spotters to live in while they scanned the horizon for enemy subs. I really doubt that Ossie and Minou would be on top of Cape Aeterna — it's too hard to get to, not private enough, and there are no services like bathrooms or fast food outlets. So that leaves the Aquarium (she could easily have traveled the fifteen miles on the free coastal

shuttle bus) but I'm even a little iffy about that.
Ossie doesn't know Nautilus as well as she knows
Windsock — where would she spend the night, or eat?
And to my knowledge, the kid doesn't have a great
deal of money — just the remains of the ten dollars
Pan gave her for ice cream and so on before she left.
My guess is that Ossie's right here in town but still,
I'd better check it out. So, donning my dark glasses
(summer is definitely here, the sun on the waves
sparkling like rhinestones) I turn onto the highway to
Nautilus to visit the whale.

There's a big controversy about this orca who
was, if you recall, the star of two Hollywood movies:
Free Willy and *Free Willy II*. After the second flick,
public outcry over his condition — he was underweight, had a droopy dorsal fin, and a most unattractive skin virus — was so great that the Nautilus
Aquarium built an immense pool for him, and a
foundation was formed to purchase him from his
too-small, too-hot pool in Mexico. The logistics of
getting the six thousand pounds of black and white
blubber from Mexico to Nautilus were pretty awe-
some, if I remember correctly, and culminated in his
being flown in a huge UPS plane, with plenty of
stops along the way to ice the guy down. He arrived
in Nautilus (the airstrip is so tiny you wouldn't
believe it) one rainy January afternoon, was loaded
onto a flatbed, and traveled the eleven miles to his
new, roomier pool past throngs of people who'd lined
the road for hours, waiting to catch a glimpse of him.

I watched the spectacle on television and for some reason I can't tell you, it brought tears to even my eyes. What was it: the prospect of all these people in a town which would have cheerfully sent out whaling boats a hundred years ago, cooperating, instead, to save one underweight orca? Or was it the prospect of maybe, just maybe, making up for kidnapping the poor creature when he was just a baby and turning him into a lonely, scrawny, warty guy who had to perform in a Mexican amusement park twice a day for the last ten years? Who knows. All I can tell you is that he now "belongs" to Nautilus, where he's as beloved as the suit-wearing, fake, giant mouse at Disneyland.

As you might expect, there are two schools of thought on the rehab and release issue, but the fact remains that the whale was the biggest thing to hit town since the tsunami of the past century. I mean, everyone has an opinion — it makes for better conversation than the weather. And whether he's ever released or not, he does seem to be a happier guy. I've gone to see him many times, and when those seven thousand pounds (he's gained a thousand since he first came) of mammal swim toward me and inspect me out of first one brown eye and then the other, I wonder if there isn't a profound intelligence there. And when I wave and he dips his snout or nose or whatever it is in response, I feel, well, awed. But, I have to admit, I feel saddened, too, because a little voice inside me whispers: *We shouldn't have done this. We shouldn't have taken him from the sea when he was a baby. It was wicked.*

I pull into the lot at the Aquarium and groan because there must be a zillion cars there, which means a zillion people, too. How am I going to spot two small girls, even if they're here?

Well, after checking out the whale's viewing windows, the puffin tank, the seal and otter pool, the shore life displays, the hands-on exhibits, the snack bar, the rest rooms, and the gift shop, I have to conclude that the girls aren't here. Hiding in a crowd is a good plan, but it must not have fit into Ossie's strategy, whatever that is. So I hustle myself back to my car and swing out onto 101, trying to remain calm as the traffic crawls toward Windsock.

Cobalt Crocus Books, just down the street from the Daily Grind, was once a run-down old house, but a total renovation and a spiffy blue and white paint job have transformed it. Anthea, the owner, is one of the circle of women one generation older than me — my late aunt's friends — with whom I never seemed to click. Maybe it's an age thing or maybe it's that I look too much like my aunt and the comparison unnerves these doughty ladies or maybe our auras aren't sympatico. I don't know, but I always feel uncomfortable around these women. Insufficient somehow. Today, Anthea, a curly-haired transplanted Californian, is on the tail end of a conversation with the UPS delivery guy, so I wait, admiring the bookstore's dynamite view of Chelsea Bay as the last of four boxes of books is signed for.

"Have you seen Ossie?" I ask as the door closes behind the brown-clad back of the UPS driver.

Anthea gives me a shrewd look and I kick myself mentally. My desperation must show. "Not since Pan brought her in to pick out a book for her birthday last week," she says. "Is something wrong?"

I consider briefly how much to tell her. "Yes and no," I equivocate. "We had a ... misunderstanding and she's temporarily missing."

Anthea raises an eyebrow, telling me that she thinks she knows what I mean, which I seriously doubt. "Want me to give you a call if I see her? I could also ask around. Discreetly."

"That would be a big help. Please do," I tell her, scribbling Kerry's car phone number down on a piece of paper. "Call the B & B and leave a message or call this number."

"She's a good kid," Anthea says. "She'll come back. Kids just go walkabout sometimes. You'll work things out."

I repress the desire to scream. "Sure," I say, and hurry outside to my car. Once there, I check Anthea off my list. I'm keeping my fingers crossed that she really will ask around because she might just turn up Ossie's location. I mean, I can't be everywhere. So, what does that leave me with ... Robin's place by the bay, the video store, and the library. And isn't there an upscale art gallery halfway to Nautilus that she likes, Trinity or Trimester or something like that? Not that she likes art, or if she does, I don't know about it, but rather that she likes the gallery's cat. Malcolm, I think its name is.

The video rental store and library are close and they're both busy, so it's easy to ask my questions about Ossie, spreading the excuse that we've just missed each other. I leave both of them with a jolly lie: "Just checking to see if she's been here. If she shows up, tell her to call home. Like E.T. Ha, ha."

Of course she won't, but I have to find out somehow if she's been hanging around, for cripe's sake.

I'm hot-footing it to my car from the video rental place when a boy with a skateboard the size of a Tomahawk missile comes after me. "Hey, wait a minute, willya?"

I turn, and the kid balances his skateboard on the concrete, leaning on it, looking around furtively. "So is Ossie in some kind of trouble?" He is, I note, about ten or eleven, all elbows and knees, and dressed in the height of coastal grunge — baggy shorts that seem to be held up by wishful thinking, an oversized black T-shirt, and a gray watch cap. His clear hazel eyes are beautiful, however, and seem to be concerned. Ossie and boys? I shudder at the thought.

"No, she's not in trouble. It's a family thing," I tell him, embellishing my lie. "An emergency. She's in town somewhere and I need to get hold of her. Now."

He burrows a finger under his watch cap to scratch what I presume is his hair and looks doubtful. "Oh. Well, the thing is, I mean I thought I saw her this morning. I get up really early to go skateboarding in the parking lots — they're empty then — and I thought I saw her with another kid. But it was so early, I, like, wondered what they were doing where they were." He waits for me to respond.

"What's your name?" I ask him, unsure of how to proceed.

"Rupert. She's a friend of mine," he says. "Ossie. We sometimes watch TV together."

"Oh yeah? What's her favorite show?"

He grins. *The X-Files.*

"Oh? I thought it was *Millenium*."

He makes a face. *"Millenium* sucks — the serial killer of the week. Chris Carter needs to get over himself."

"Okay, you pass." Maybe it's his pretty hazel eyes, or the fact that he knows something about Ossie or his assertion that he cares, but I decide to trust him. A little. "Rupert, help me here — where did you see Ossie?"

"The office that burned down last year, you know, that PI's place on the hill. The one they're putting a new roof on. Ossie and this other kid were just, like, leaving. That was right after the sun came up. About six."

I almost smite myself on the forehead. That PI's place on the hill is — ta, da — Kerry's office. Of course Ossie would go there. She knew it was safe and deserted, and she probably figured she'd have all the time she needed to find a way in. I'm almost laughing now, because Kerry will croak when I tell her where the kids spent last night. Oh man, this should be a piece of cake. With any luck, we can get into Kerry's place, hide, and scoop Ossie and Minou up when they try to sneak in tonight. And then where can we stash them that's absolutely safe? I groan and Rupert looks at me anxiously.

"Are you okay? I mean you're not sick or anything, are you? Do you have, like, a virus? Something communicable? Is that why you're trying to find Ossie? Wow — that's the family emergency, isn't it. She's spreading something. Wow." His eyebrows disappear up under his cap.

Young Rupert has written a whole *X-Files* scenario here in the space of ten seconds and I have all I can do to keep up with him. "No!" I yell. "No one's sick!"

"Okay, okay," he says soothingly, but judging from the sparkle in his eyes, he doesn't believe me. "Chill."

"Rupert, what you can do for us, for Ossie, is to get on that skateboard of yours and wheel around town. See if you can spot her. And the kid she's with."

He nods solemnly. "And don't approach too closely."

"What?"

"In case the bug is airborne, I'm not to approach too closely, right?"

"Oh jeez." What the hell — if the kid wants to believe in a contagion on the loose in Windsock, so be it. As long as he cooperates. "Okay, just in case, don't get too close. Okay?"

"Uh, huh," he says, settling his watch cap more firmly on his head in preparation for blast-off.

"You got that?"

"Yeah, sure, I got it."

"Call me at the B & B," I yell after him. "Let me know if you see her!"

He waves a skinny hand, gets his board up to speed and jets off, shorts and shirt flapping in the breeze, intent on his mission.

I cruise slowly through Windsock on my way to Robin's little yellow house by the bay, looking carefully at every group of kids I see. And they're seemingly everywhere. I mean, school is out and what do kids have to do but hang out? So they're in clumps in the parking lot at Roy's Supermarket, in bunches outside the so-called Youth Center, in groups at the school — surely a sad testament to kids' imaginative abilities if they can't think of anywhere better to spend their summer vacation than the steps of the local school. And our future is in the hands of such as these? I shudder, preferring to think that my future will be in the hands of quirky kids like the loyal Ossie or the unquenchably imaginative Rupert.

By the time I get to the bay, I've examined enough kids to make me think the human race is de-evolving and I'm in a state of despair. The girls at least look clean, but the boys — jeez. They look far worse than Rupert because whereas he had the grunge look down pat, he's clearly bathed in recent memory. A lot of these kids look really and truly grungy. I try to remember what the guys looked like when I was in junior high and can't. I mean, they just looked normal. The surfer look, the preppy look. Of course, that was California and everyone wore shorts and T-shirts so maybe that's not a fair comparison. But this marriage between ultra-baggy gangsta and Northwest grunge has produced a very unattractive offspring indeed. Poor guys.

And another thing — whenever I see one of these not-so-young kids looking like they've just stepped out of someone's nightmare, I always wonder who'll hire them. I've had several of them stop by the B & B and ask me for work and I'd love to hire someone to cut my lawns or trim my trees or haul away yard debris, but my guests would faint dead away if they ever clapped eyes on them.

To be fair, we don't have many of these baggy

boys here on the coast — Rupert will find that he'll be moving on to Levis, white T-shirts, and backwards baseball caps all too soon. Then, when he graduates from or drops out of high school, he can look forward to turning his baseball cap around, getting a six-dollar-an-hour job at one of the local gas stations, buying a gun rack for his pickup, drinking beer in the woods on Saturday night with his buddies, marrying his high school girlfriend (who will then be pregnant), and voting Republican. Well, maybe Ossie can work on him. Anyone who likes *The X-Files* and fantasizes about diseases on the loose in Windsock deserves a better fate.

I'm starving, so I park my car, grab some fish and chips from Coastal Seafoods — Kerry's aunt's seafood restaurant which is just a few doors down from Robin's Metamorphosis Center — and sit in the sun, looking out at the bay and thinking. Now that Rupert's told me what he has, I'm sure that the kids are somewhere in town. Why would they go anywhere else when they can spend the nights in comfort and safety at Kerry's place? The question is, where are they spending their days? I close my eyes, trying to imagine what I would do if I were Ossie. Well, I'd hide. And then I'd take Minou to Nautilus. But where would I hide, dammit? Windsock is a tiny town, just a smidgen bigger than Lavner Bay.

Think, I tell myself. Think. Ossie wouldn't want to be seen coming and going from Kerry's — Rupert's spotting her was just bad luck. So wherever she was going, she'd need to get there fast, before the town (or, for all she knew, Remy) was stirring. Which means what? That wherever she's hiding out is close to Kerry's? The Metamorphosis Center, where I am now, is just too darned far away. Or is it? With a sigh, I decide I'd better go on in and ask Robin if she's seen Ossie. But I'm amazed at how badly I don't want to. It's not that Robin isn't a cool person to talk to, but I've already bared my soul to her once this week. Twice seems a little, well, much. Besides, once again, I'll have to lie about the fact that I've lost Ossie.

I toss the last of my fries to the ever-hungry gulls, stuff my trash in a dumpster, and reluctantly head across the parking lot to the Metamorphosis Center. Unlatching the gate, I walk up the cobblestone path and up the steps onto the porch. But with a mixture of relief and disappointment, I see that there's a note taped to the door that says: CLOSED UNTIL FRIDAY. PLEASE CALL THEN. Okay, that's that, I think, and sit on the top step of the porch, absently looking out at the bay.

And then it hits me — Ossie's favorite hangouts have cats. Frog Hollow, Few Mornings, the Metamorphosis Center, the video rental store . . . and Trillium Gallery or whatever the hell it's called. Is this significant? I don't know, but I feel that I'd certainly better check it out.

Chapter 14

Trillium Gallery, which I've never visited because I don't understand and am thoroughly intimidated by modern art, has a life-sized indigo neon horse grazing in front of one of its windows. That, combined with its wave-like cedar architecture, have convinced me that this is a place I don't belong. But when Malcolm, a friendly Maine coon cat, greets me at the door and takes me inside, I see that perhaps I was too hasty. There's a tall, slender, short-haired blonde wearing black pants and a lavender shirt and a shorter, older, dark-haired woman sporting a cheerful floral dress and a button that says WE LOVE OUR GAY AND LESBIAN CHILDREN. My jaw almost drops but I recover nicely. Having delivered me to this pair, Malcolm saunters off to a far corner of the gallery.

I clear my throat nervously, ill at ease despite the dark-haired woman's reassuring button. "I'm Allison O'Neil," I begin. "I own Lavner Bay B & B."

"Coral Agnes," says the woman with the button. "You must be Grace's niece. You look like her."

"Lindsay Corder," says the blonde, eyeing me speculatively. Eve would be happy to know that my dyke radar is pinging like mad. On the blonde, not the brunette. I mean, I had the button for a clue, didn't I?

"I'm looking for Pan's daughter, Ossie," I explain. "I, er, need her and I was in the vicinity and wondered if she might be here."

Lindsay looks at me oddly. "The last time I saw her was last week. She came to see Malcolm."

So, as I guessed, it isn't the art that draws Ossie, it's the cat.

"Is everything okay?" she asks.

No, I want to say, everything is not okay. In fact, everything is very much not okay and I have only a day to make it okay and after what Kerry's told me I'm scared to death that it may never be okay again. But I force myself to smile and nod. "Yeah, everything's okay."

"You know," Lindsay says thoughtfully, "if you're looking for Ossie, you might try her teacher."

"Her teacher? But school's out."

"Yes, it is, but Suzanna's a friend of mine and I've heard her speak often of Ossie. She thinks she's an exceptional little girl. And I know they keep in touch over the summer break — Suzanna's going to take some of the kids on a camping trip in August. So maybe try her."

"Thanks," I tell her. "I really appreciate this."

"No problem," she assures me. "Say, how about coming to our reception Friday night? We have two new artists whose work we're installing — a fiber artist and a glassmaker — and we'd love to see you. Everyone comes to our receptions," she says encouragingly.

"Bring a friend if you like," says Coral. "Bring three or four. We always have lots of good eats."

"Um, er, thanks, maybe I will," I mumble, almost tripping over Malcolm who has come to twine between, then sit on my feet. I bend down to pat him, wondering if I have the guts to, you know, socialize. With others of my ilk. But an art reception? Me? With a friend? Yikes. Well, maybe. But first we'll have to see what the morrow brings.

Suzanna, I recall from reading the local fish wrapper, is teaching a writing class at one of our used bookstores this month. Over-the-Waves Books in Lavner Bay, if I remember rightly. At the drive-through espresso hut in Sea Lion Rock, I order a latte and sip it as I head south, cursing the ponderous pachyderm of a motor home plunked squarely in my path. In a moment or two, an apple core, a banana peel, and a couple of paper coffee cups are tossed from the motor home into the ditch.

"Litterer!" I yell impotently, moved to fury and

honking by the behemoth's California plates. "You trashed your state and now you want to trash ours!" And then I cool my jets because, really, who am I to yell? I've been here what, ten months? I'm hardly a native. Still, I do a slow burn all the way south through Windsock and into Lavner Bay where, thankfully, the California litterwagon turns off at a state park. Could it be, however, that I've become proprietary of my new state? Protective even? Yikes.

A quick stop at the B & B reassures me that the place is still standing. It's well after lunch now and the departing guests have checked out, leaving us with two rooms available. The industrious Eve has laundered the sheets and towels, cleaned the toilets (hurray!), vacuumed and dusted, and generally gotten the rooms ready. I'm impressed.

"We had a call from two women in Cannon Beach," she tells me. "They heard of the place and wanted to know if we had any rooms. I said yes and took their VISA card numbers to guarantee the rooms. Was that okay?"

"That was fine," I tell her. "Did you tell them they need to be here or cancel by five o'clock?"

She nods.

"Okay. If I'm not back by then and they don't show, don't charge their VISA cards — they'll probably get in later." She starts to say something and I hold up my hand. "We hold their rooms for them until we lock the doors at nine. That's when we charge their VISA cards, because they've screwed us up — we could have rented those rooms. If they call and cancel, don't charge their VISA cards, but go ahead and rent the rooms." She looks doubtful, and I can see that if she becomes proprietress, she'll rule with a heavier hand. Well, she's welcome to do so, but she'll get a bad rep. I believe in giving people lots of time to get here — a romantic dinner in Flotsam or Moose Bay can take hours longer than you'd planned. And the traffic on 101 in the summer is excruciatingly slow, which makes getting anyplace on time a white-knuckle experience.

"Oh, a fax came for you," she says as I'm on my way out, handing me a sheaf of paper about as thick as a city phone directory. I have no idea what it might be so I sit down on the couch to look it over before I realize one, it's for Kerry and two, it's Remy LePlante's rap sheet. I read on, mesmerized, horrified, and elated all at once because the little slimebag has hardly spent a month out of prison since he was eighteen. Petty theft, larceny, embezzlement, check forgery — all this before he was twenty. Then it seems he progressed to a whole different level of criminality — drug dealing, pimping, burglary, gambling. I sit back, thinking, noticing the fact that none of his crimes involved violence — might Remy be a little bit of a coward? Reading quickly now, I come to the last page . . . and hoot with glee! The little weasel is wanted on an outstanding warrant in Florida — he jumped bail!

"Yes!" I yell, frightening Sammy, who races upstairs, tail the size of a salami.

Crossing to the desk, I dial Kerry's cell phone number and, when she answers, blurt out my discovery.

"Kerry, you won't believe it. A fax came for you. It's Remy's rap sheet and he's a wanted man!"

"He is?"

"Florida wants him. It seems he made bail on the latest of his escapades and then disappeared."

I can hear her yelling and I hope it's with excitement at what I've told her. With these hordes of California drivers on the roads, you never know. "This is great," she says, confirming my hopes. "I'll call Belcher and Johanssen. See if they'll pick him up."

"And I found out something else pretty interesting," I tell her smugly. "Ossie and Minou spent the night at your place."

"At . . ." I can hear the question in her voice.

"Yeah. At your place. At your home-cum-office. The one that's being re-roofed. The one you abandoned to come and seek shelter with me."

"No kidding," she says, admiration in her voice. "In that case, I'm going to give up running around Nautilus and come on back. If they spent last night at my place, chances are that they figure they can spend tonight there, too. I mean, it's safe and they're not likely to be disturbed. We'll pay a call on them tonight and bring them home. The question is, where are they now? And where's Remy? I'd sure hate for them to cross paths."

"I think Ossie's pretty smart," I say tentatively. "I think she's probably done the best she could to keep Minou safe, but I agree with you — what if Remy gets to them before we can?"

"Exactly," she says softly. "How'd you do in Windsock? Any leads?"

"I was just on my way out to talk to someone who might know something," I tell her. "Why don't I do that and meet you back here."

"Okay," she says, then, "Allison?"

"Yeah?"

"Stay away from my place until we can go tonight, okay? We don't want to spook them. By the way, how'd you find that particular piece of information?"

"Tell you when I see you."

As I leave, Eve is sitting on the couch in the lobby, writing in her journal, Sammy sprawled out by her side, giving me his *Nyah, nyah, you never let me on the couch but I've found a sucker who will* look. I wonder what she's writing — a recounting of her experiences as an apprentice hotelier? A mournful tribute to the departed Katherine? A mystery set on the Oregon coast? A haiku? I close the door quietly on the two of them and head out for Over-the-Waves Books.

At the bookstore, a writing class is in progress in the large inner room, so I station myself in the small outer one, the one with the coffee and cookies, the mysteries and the cat beds (I'd momentarily forgotten that the owner has two working cats) and, taking a Caitlin Reece mystery off the shelf, prepare to wait. I don't have long. In ten minutes or so, a horde of eager would-be writers emerges, papers and books in hand. What an assortment — no-nonsense dowdy dowagers; dewy-eyed, braided, Mexican-skirted, Ophelia types; slender, tweedy young men with spectacles and bad skin. I never dreamed that so many people wanted to learn to write. I mean, what can all these folks have to say that's so important that they want to share it with the rest of us? But then, I guess I ought to be grateful that someone's teaching them the difference between foreshadowing and foreplay. Otherwise folks like the bookstore owner, not to mention yours truly, would be out of business. In a minute, I'm able to buttonhole Suzanna — a middle-aged, motherly woman with an open, friendly face, glasses, and dark hair turning to gray (courtesy of her students no doubt) and we walk outside to the back porch.

"I'll just take a minute of your time," I say, having already decided to tell her, well, certainly not everything, but a lot of the truth. "I'm Allison O'Neil — I own Lavner Bay Bed and Breakfast. Pan left Ossie with me while she went back east and well, we had a misunderstanding. Ossie's missing."

Suzanna gives me a long, critical look. "I know. She showed up on my doorstep this morning with another girl."

I'm so relieved I almost faint. "Oh man, oh brother, you don't know how happy that makes me. I was so worried about her."

Suzanna's lips compress into a thin, disapproving line. "Ossie specifically asked me not to call you or talk to you if you came around asking questions."

"What?"

"She explained to me that you'd want to try to reunite Minou with her father and, well, she told me quite a story. Miss O'Neil, if even half of it is true, the child needs to leave town with her mother, don't you think? The last thing she needs is to be placed in the care of her father."

144

I'm so mad I feel myself start to turn red — I can't help it, never could. "I'm afraid you don't have all the facts here," I start, but she turns to me icily.

"Anyone who threatens to turn a child over to Attila the Hun in order to gain peace and quiet ought not to have custody of that child," she pronounces, arms crossed over her breasts, eyes blazing. "Even temporarily."

"Like I said, you don't have all the facts here," I attempt to point out. "And for that matter, we don't know if the story Minou's telling us is true!" She opens her mouth to start in again and I shush her with an upraised hand. "Oh, it may well be — I've just seen the father's rap sheet and he certainly hasn't been a choirboy — but that doesn't mean that reuniting the kid with her mother is a guarantee of her well-being. I mean, how do you think the happy family came to be reunited on the coast in the first place?"

"I — what do you mean?" Suzanna asks.

"Well, according to a friend of Alyce's, Remy was here first, and Alyce only came to join him after he begged hard enough. As in I love you, I want you, I need you, do wop de do. Life must be an oldies tune for Alyce. Besides," I sigh, deciding to level with her, "Alyce won't be making bail and going home with Minou. If she's lucky, she'll get a minimum sentence and do sixteen months in prison. Minou will go to CPS who may or may not elect to send her home to her relatives."

There are a couple of lawn chairs on the deck and she collapses in one. "This is a dysfuctional mess!" she exclaims, looking at me accusingly.

145

"Hey, I didn't cause it," I tell her. "Neither did Ossie. I think both of us — and you, too — are in the middle of a no-win thing."

"What do you mean?"

I'm glad she asked that question because it gives me the chance to talk out my fears and frustration. "Okay. Here's what I think is likely to happen. Alyce is tied up so tight with Remy that she can't break loose. It's another one of those top forty things — only country and western this time. And poor Minou is in the middle. With Ossie. Minou's going to get her heart broken and Ossie's going to feel hurt and betrayed, and that's the least that's likely to happen." I'm well into it and I have to pace up and down the deck a little to disperse energy. "Remy's wanted on a bail violation in Florida and we can probably get him picked up for that, but what I'm afraid of is the timing of all this. I mean, can we have it wrapped up by tomorrow? Only if we're very lucky. Remy's out there somewhere and if he's able to get his hands on Minou, he'll probably be able to grab Ossie at the same time. And if that happens, we may never get the kids back." There, I've said it, and now that I have, it's finally real. A little voice of panic starts yammering in a back room of my brain and before it completely paralyzes me, I slam its door. *I'll deal with you later,* I tell it.

Suzanna puts her hands over her face. Clearly this is a plot that none of her fledgling writers ever suggested. "But what can we do?"

"What can we do? Easy. We can see that Remy doesn't get to the kids. We don't know where Remy is but we do know where the kids are." I look at her, willing her to tell. "Don't we?"

She nods. "As far as I know, they're at my place. I told them they could stay there and watch TV and so on, eat lunch, and that I'd be home for supper and we could talk then."

My stomach contracts in apprehension. "Oh yeah? What did you tell them you'd talk about?"

"Well, about what to do. About going to the police. About getting, well, professional help."

I groan. Ossie's way too smart for that. She knows as well as I do that the so-called professional help in our county is not likely to listen to a couple of kids and that even if they did, their help might well be too late. I have to hand it to her — she's one hell of a good protector. But even her enterprising spirit might not be enough.

"What's wrong?" Suzanna wants to know.

"I think Ossie will try to take care of this herself. I wouldn't be at all surprised if the kids are gone when you get back."

She's really alarmed now. "But where would they go?"

I look appropriately thoughtful, and the lie comes easily to my lips. "I don't know, Suzanna." Of course I know, but no way am I going to play my trump card.

"But, it'll be night soon. Where *could* they go?" By now she's actually wringing her hands.

"Go home," I tell her. "If they're at your place, call me. I'll be at the B & B. If they're not there, stay there. Maybe they'll come back. Or call you. Ossie trusts you," I remind her. She nods. "Oh," I ask her as she stands up, looking bewildered. "Ossie has a friend named Rupert. I want to talk to him. Do you happen to know his last name?"

147

"Staples," she says distractedly. "He lives with his mother. They're in the phone book. I'd better go now, Miss O'Neil. The girls may still be at my place."

"They probably are," I say soothingly as she hurries away. But that's just for her benefit. I'd bet the B & B that they're long gone.

Chapter 15

So, I'm heading back to the B & B, about as depressed as I've been in a long time. As I've said, I'm willing to bet the farm that the kids won't be at Suzanna's — her talk of professionals and cops wouldn't have convinced Ossie, who's seen one too many cop movies for her own good. Or has she? Does art reflect life or vice versa? Who knows anymore? And, I ponder as I drive home, The Oss undoubtedly knows, as do I and everyone who reads the local cat-box liner, that both our law enforcement officers are several logs short of a jam. After all, Johanssen alone has seven (count them) lawsuits filed against him by people ranging from city employees (the old roving hand syndrome) to members of the public (the excessive force thing). Yep. If I were Ms. Ocelot Constantine, I might tend to trust my own wiles, too.

The sun's setting as I pull up to the B & B, noting with some relief that Kerry's truck is already there. Eve catches my eye as I come inside.

"Kerry's on the back deck," she says, looking rested, professional, and cheerful — every bit the hotelier.

I can't, I absolutely can't deal with Eve, so I frantically search my brain for a place to temporarily banish her. "Listen, you need to go and have some supper," I say. "I may have to be out tonight and, well, you need a break."

"Okay," she says agreeably. "Is the Chowder Vat down the road any good?"

"Yeah, it is. Any problems here?"

"Not a one. The two women who called are checked in so we're full again."

"Any phone calls for me?" I ask, hoping against hope that Suzanna called to say that Ossie and Minou are there.

"Nope," she says, picking up her things and heading out the door, presumably to beam upon the denizens of the Chowder Vat. "I'll get takeout and be right back," she assures me. "I know you need me here."

I feel so depressed that I temporarily consider breaking out the bottle of Canadian Club that Bradley gave me for a going-away present, but sanity prevails and I pour myself a glass of milk instead. There's nothing much to eat but some leftover tuna casserole, so I pop that in the microwave, and when the concoction is hot, dump it into a bowl.

"What's up?" I ask Kerry, balancing my snack in both hands and closing the kitchen door behind me with my foot.

She's sitting there in the twilight, feet up on the deck rail, drinking a Diet Coke. "Not much, white girl," she says, sounding as disconsolate as I feel. I note that she's changed into jeans, a dark T-shirt and sneakers, presumably in preparation for the night's activities.

"What's the matter with us?" I ask her. "We're going to go get the kids anytime now, right?"

"Right."

"And we'll stash them someplace safe until tomorrow, right?"

"Yup."

"Have we figured out where?"

"Yeah. I'll call my cousin Daniel," she says. "He'll take them home with him. His house is on Indian land. Remy wouldn't dare follow Daniel onto the reservation."

"That sounds like a good plan."

"Yup."

"So why do we sound so funereal?"

She drains her Coke and sets the can down beside her chair. "Maybe because we're both having the same bad feelings about this."

My tuna turns to lead in my stomach and I put the remains of dinner down by her Coke can. "I know. I've been feeling it ever since I drove up to the B & B. What's going on?"

"It's the BOC factor," she says after a moment.

"The what?"

"The BOC factor — Beyond Our Control. There are too many things that could go wrong. Or if you have a more poetic turn of mind, you might call it the What If factor. What if Remy grabs the kids before we get to him? What if he has help? What if there's a shootout? What if one of us gets hurt? Or one of them? What if he already has them?"

Mouth dry, I look at my watch. It's well after seven. "Think the roofing crew has gone yet?"

"Yeah," she says, "but I don't think the kids will show up at my place until it's dark. They won't want anyone seeing them. Let's give it another hour."

"Have you talked to Daniel about this?"

"Yeah. He'll be ready to roll when I call him."

"So there's nothing to do but wait."

"Yup."

I finish my milk and think again about the Canadian Club. Nah. Maybe later. Suddenly something occurs to me and it's such an exciting idea that I blurt it right out.

"Kerry, didn't you tell me that you have friends on the Nautilus police force?"

"Yeah."

"Oh, jeez. I just thought of something. Listen, we think Remy's in Nautilus, not Windsock or Lavner Bay, right?"

"So?"

"So, listen. Can't you call one of your friends in the Nautilus PD and have *him* look for Remy? I mean, I don't know exactly how this works, but don't law enforcement agencies cooperate to pick up bad guys wanted on out-of-state warrants?"

"Yeah," she says slowly.

"So, wouldn't Tallahassee be overjoyed to know where Remy is?"

She says nothing and I'm embarrassed now, afraid that she'll think it was a pretty lame suggestion, brought on by my reading too many cops-and-robbers stories. But I might as well blunder ahead, I figure. "I mean if Florida wants him, we — well, you really — could call the Tallahassee cops and get *them* to call the Nautilus PD and get Remy picked up. Couldn't you?"

She shrugs. "Why not give it a try? In theory it should help us. Worst case is that it wouldn't hurt. I'll fax Tallahassee and alert my friend in the Nautilus PD to watch for a reply."

I follow her inside, and as I start putting the dishes in the sink and rinsing them off, I hear the front door open and a murmur of voices in the lobby. I stick my head around the corner to find Eve provocatively perched on the reception desk, quite close to Kerry who, if I remember correctly, is trying to compose a fax to send to the Tallahassee Police Department where it will be the middle of the night and she'll have a hell of a time trying to convince anyone of anything. She flashes me a beseeching look and I rescue her from the wiles of Eve.

"So, how was the Chowder Vat?" I inquire, hands in the pockets of my jeans, sashaying slowly out of the kitchen like a black widow spider on the prowl. I look proprietarily at Kerry, giving Eve my best hands-off look, and finally she gets it, leaping guiltily off the desk and taking one long step away from Kerry.

"Er, busy. But I got a bowl of takeout chowder as

you suggested. Sourdough bread, too. Want some?" she offers. "It's hot."

I raise an eyebrow and she blushes furiously. "No thanks, we've eaten," I say, feigning one last smoldering glance at Kerry. "You can go on into the kitchen and put that in a real bowl," I tell her, and she's so evidently nonplused that she just goes. Hmmf, I say to myself. Pretty feeble effort for a vamp.

Kerry hangs up the phone, looks past me at Eve's retreating back, and gives a sort of shudder. "Time to go," she says, grabbing her red anorak from the coat rack and pulling it over her head.

I find my purple fleece jacket where I've thrown it over a chair and call to Eve. "We're out of here. Just lock up behind us, okay? And make sure Sammy stays in."

"Okay," I hear faintly from the kitchen and as I recall the guilty look on Eve's face, I have to work really, really hard not to laugh. Because if I do, I'm afraid that I'll never stop.

Chapter 16

It's pitch dark, and there's a thunderstorm
building out over the ocean, forked tongues of
lightning illuminating the sky far out to sea. The
positive ions or whatever are making me as nervous
as a cat on hot bricks and I'm having a hard time
even sitting still. It's maybe an eight-mile drive from
the B & B to Kerry's place, and I fidget every yard
of the way.

"Should we park at Hamburger Heaven and
walk?" I ask Kerry. "We don't want your truck to
spook them."

She thinks this over. "You know, if I were the kids, I'd be less spooked if a truck drove up than if I heard someone scrabbling in the dark at the back door."

"You're probably right," I agree. "But one of us needs to take the back of your place and one the front, just so they don't have a chance to run off. And we need to announce ourselves loudly —"

Kerry puts a hand on my arm. "We will. Take three deep breaths. Calm down."

"Sorry. I just don't want anything to go wrong."

"It won't. Okay, we're almost there. D'you want the front or the back?"

"Front. You take the back. And —"

"Announce myself loudly. I will."

Kerry turns into the parking lot in front of her office/house, lets me out, and quickly shuts off the engine, jumping out of the truck and running around to the back entrance. Shining my flashlight on the piles of roofing shingles, I pick my way through the maze and finally reach the front door.

"Ossie, Minou, it's Allison," I yell. "I'm coming in. Don't be scared — everything's okay. But don't try to run off, either. There are a couple of things you need to know." I fumble the key into the lock and after a few tries, get the door open. Lights go on in the back of the house and for a moment I'm overcome with relief — Kerry's found the girls and everything's okay. But then she comes through the doorway alone, and my heart heads for my shoes.

"No one in the back," she says, reaching for the light switch to flood this room — the one she uses as her office — with illumination. "They've been here," she says. "They used some blankets and pillows and slept on the floor in my spare room, but no one's here now."

"Well, maybe we're too early," I say, knowing how eager I sound. "Maybe they haven't made it here yet."

"Yeah, maybe," she says, doubtful. "But there are a couple of dishes in the sink that are still gummy with spaghetti. Looks like they ate dinner not too long ago."

"Dammit, where are they?" I wail. "And why did they leave? This was a safe place for them. What happened?"

"Come look for yourself," she says and I follow her into the back. "No signs of a struggle, dishes piled neatly in the sink, sleeping bags rolled up."

"Dammit!" I yell, just because I have to say something.

Thunder rumbles off to the west and Kerry crosses to the window to look outside. "It's going to rain pretty soon. They'll need to get inside somewhere. Why don't you call Ossie's friend — the kid with the skateboard you told me about. I'll get the truck out of here just in case they do show up. And let's turn the lights out. Make everything look the way they're accustomed to seeing it."

It's bad enough as Kerry moves from room to room, turning off lights, plunging us suddenly into darkness. But then, without a word, she slips outside into the night, leaving me alone. Hey, wait, I want to call, but of course I don't. Her truck's headlights sweep across the walls once, and then I'm plunged into darkness again and I find myself shivering, fantasizing that she's leaving me here by myself in the middle of the biggest mess I've ever been in. I mean, what *will* I tell Pan if things go badly? Get a grip, I tell myself. Things will work out. They have to. Calm down.

I dial Rupert's house and a squeaky pre-adolescent voice answers. "Heaven — God speaking."

I'm enraged. "Does your mother know you answer the phone like that?"

"Er, no," a voice I recognize as Rupert's answers. "I was expecting someone else. So, um, who's this?"

"Allison O'Neil."

Silence.

"I own the B & B. Remember?"

"Oh yeah, sure."

"Did you see Ossie today?"

"Nope," he says, a note of something I can't place in his voice.

"Rupert, please tell me the truth. This is very important. I have to find her before tomorrow morning. I absolutely, positively have to."

"I am telling you the truth. I didn't see her. I swear."

There's something he's not telling me and that something's making me crazy. I briefly consider telling him everything, just to impress upon him how necessary honesty is, and then I remind myself that maybe Ossie's done just that and maybe that's why he isn't being honest. Oh brother.

"I'm here at Kerry-the-PI's place, waiting for her," I tell him. "Can you think of any reason why she wouldn't come back here tonight?"

"Um, well, no," he says. "Not offhand."

"Oh, Rupert," I say, trying my best not to burst into tears. "I know you think you're protecting her and her friend, but she's needs more help than you can give her. More help than I can give her, too."

"Look, I told you I didn't see her," he says, aggravation in his voice. "Don't you believe me?"

"Yeah, sure," I say, discouraged because clearly nothing I can say is going to budge him. "Will you do something for me? Will you write these phone numbers down?"

"Okay," he agrees grudgingly.

I give him Kerry's office and car phone numbers, making him repeat them, which pisses him off even more. "I'll be here all night. Please call me if you, well, think of anything. I'm Ossie's friend, Rupert. I just want her to be safe."

"I'm her friend, too," he says ambiguously. "I'll call if I, you know, think of anything."

I hang up the phone, put my head in my arms, and give in to my desire to cry. "Dammit!" I wail, wanting to kick the walls down.

"What's wrong?" Kerry says, coming in the front door and shining her light on me.

"What is this — an interrogation? Turn that damned flashlight off!" I blubber. "That little shit knows something but he won't tell me." I jump to my feet. "I'm going over there and beat it out of him. I'm —"

"Whoa, now," Kerry says reasonably, interposing herself between me and the door. "You're not going anywhere in that frame of mind."

"Oh yeah, who says?" I ask her, over the edge now. "You?"

"Yeah, me."

"Ha!" I say, giving her a shove.

"Allison," she says slowly, not budging. "Calm down."

"Get the fuck out of my way!"

She shakes her head. "No. I won't."

"Then I'll just have to make you," I tell her, taking a swing at her head. She sidesteps and comes up behind me, grabbing me and pinning my arms to my sides. This makes me crazier than I am and I stomp on her foot, hurting her, making her curse under her breath. We lurch around the room like a couple of drunks, me squirming and yelling, her hanging on, until finally I'm all fought out and there's nothing left to do but cry. "Let me go," I sniffle.

"Promise you won't do anything stupid?" she asks.

This strikes me as so funny that I start to laugh, but it goes up or comes down the wrong pipe and I start hiccuping in between bouts of crying. "No, I can't promise that," I say, "but I can promise that I won't try to take any more swings at you or go beat up adolescent boys."

"Okay." She lets me go. "Okay."

I feel like a fool. "So where did you learn to handle hysterical females?" I ask her. "From Daniel?" She shakes her head and I kick myself because I've stepped in it again. But this time I don't care. I mean, I'm so exhausted I could lie down here on the floor and sleep for a week. "I told Rupert that I'd be here all night. It's probably wishful thinking, but maybe the kids will come back. Oh, hell. I can't think of anything else to do. I'm going to sack out on the sleeping bags they used and wait for them."

Using my flashlight as little as possible, I find my way to Kerry's spare room and, feeling about eighty-five, unroll one of the sleeping bags which have been neatly piled in the corner. I have the sense that Kerry's standing there in the dark, just outside the storeroom door, and for one brief moment I consider trying to talk to her about that ill-considered hysterical females remark I made, but then I lie down, sigh once, and the world slips out from under me.

Chapter 17

It's one of those mornings when you don't want to open your eyes because you know there's something unimaginably horrible in store for you — a geometry test you haven't studied for, or Prom Night (and you have a date with your best friend's brother, not your best friend), or a trip to the gynecologist. I open my eyes, recognize nothing, and panic for a moment until I manage to orient myself: Kerry's spare room, Windsock, and (worse yet) Tuesday morning. Then I really freak out because if it's Tuesday morning and I'm lying here, then the kids didn't come back. Heart hammering, I stagger to my feet, feeling as though I really did consume a significant portion of that bottle of Canadian Club, but unless I was abducted by and partied with aliens, I know I didn't.

"Morning," Kerry says, appearing in the doorway. For one giddy instant I'm sure she's been standing there all night but then I realize that no of course she hasn't. Knowing Kerry, I'm sure she very sensibly got some sleep in her own bed, had a shower and (probably) breakfast, donned clean clothes, and is now ready for a new day. Whereas I feel and probably look as though I've been pulled through a knothole backwards. She has a cup of what I hope is coffee in her hands and as she offers it to me, I try not to grab.

"It's almost six-thirty," she says. "The roofers will probably be here soon so I thought we'd want to leave before they arrive."

"Good idea," I mutter. "Where's the bathroom?"

Kerry points down the hall and I struggle to my feet. Neither of us is talking about what didn't happen last night — the kids didn't come back. "There are clean towels in the cabinet," she says. "You can take a shower if you want. There's a brand new toothbrush in the lefthand cabinet drawer — my dentist always gives me complimentary ones," she explains. "Floss, too. And I have some clean socks and T-shirts and things like that if you like. We're probably about the same size. I've left them for you."

Amazed, I take my coffee into the bathroom, close the door and shed my now-disgusting clothes. On the back of the bathroom door is a blue and white striped terrycloth robe with the word HERS

163

embroidered in navy over one breast. I puzzle over this for a full minute before it hits me: what Smiling Eve was getting at is true. I mean this robe, and all the spare toothbrushes and floss and so on. Kerry's amazingly well set up for overnight guests. Yikes. As I shampoo, I try hard to put this new information about Kerry into focus. It's a little like finding out your best friend, about whom you thought you knew most things, is a closet Buddhist or a stock market whiz or reads ancient Greek.

As I towel myself dry and climb into Kerry's underwear (a brand new pair of turquoise Haines for Her bikini briefs), don a pair of Kerry's socks (blue and white cotton Ragg), and put on one of her T-shirts (a faded, soft, blue one), I tell myself that none of us really knows anything about each other. I mean, Eve could still be wrong. Kerry could just be a Virgo — always well prepared.

"Ready," I tell Kerry, as I emerge from the bathroom. "Let's go." I note she's dressed down a little today — same jeans as yesterday, but a faded yellow T-shirt and Nikes instead of her usual Dockers and Birkenstocks. "You're looking casual," I comment.

She looks down at her jeans. "Just a feeling. I mean, I called my friend in the Nautilus PD and supposedly they'll be there ready for Remy, but what if they aren't?" She slips into a black leather jacket and stuffs a pair of handcuffs into her back pocket. "I'm going to be ready," she says, reinforcing my suspicion that she's a Virgo. "This guy isn't getting away."

"Wow," I say, feeling more than a little apprehensive but my apprehension is nothing compared with what I feel when she unlocks a drawer in her desk and pulls out a gun, holster, and belt clip. "Um, er," I say as she affixes it to the back of her jeans.

"I have a license for the gun if that's what you're worried about. And I know how to use it."

"I, well, okay. If you say so."

She takes a pair of sunglasses from the same drawer and suddenly we're ready. "Let's go," she says.

"Okay," I agree, possibly more frightened than I've ever been in my life. "Okay."

So here we are sitting in Kerry's truck by the sidewalk outside the Nautilus courthouse, City Hall, and jail — a four-story red brick building built around a charming grassy courtyard with planters filled with yellow and orange marigolds. There's a bus shelter directly in our line of vision, which means we can't see worth a rat's ass. A light rain starts, misting the windows, and I realize I have to go to the bathroom.

"Where the hell are they?" Kerry fumes, looking up and down the street and I hope she means her Nautilus PD friends, but she might mean Remy and the LA movie producers. "It's almost nine o'clock. Alyce is first on the docket." And then I realize she probably means the girls and my heart sinks. Where the hell *are* the girls? "One of us will have to go inside."

"Me," I volunteer. "I have to find a bathroom. I'll do that and then go on into the courtroom."

"Bathroom's on the left, and the courtroom you want is on the right."

I sprint through the rain, up the stairs, through

the metal detector, and into the bathroom where I get rid of my three cups of coffee, and check under every cubicle door for small feet. Nada. Taking three deep breaths I exit the bathroom and find myself in the middle of a gaggle of jurors, attorneys, and assorted court officials. They're all headed down the hall to Courtroom Two so I try to swim against the tide and make my way back to Courtroom One. And that's when I see him. Remy. He's got on a white shirt and tie, well-fitting black trousers and loafers, and is carrying a bunch of papers. He even has less goop on his hair. It's a pretty good disguise. I would have missed him in all the bustle in the hall — he looks every bit the part of some sleazy public defender. But then he turns around and I see it's the same Remy — mean little eyes, bad skin, slash of a mouth. I step behind the bulk of a bailiff before Remy can spot me and when I peek out, he's still following the crowd into Courtroom Two.

I hurry back down the hall toward Courtoom One, deciding I'll take just a peek inside. A Nautilus PD officer gives me a no-running-in-the-halls look and I pull open the big doors, praying to see the kids. But of course they're not there. Apart from the judge, a row of prisoners in bright orange jumpsuits, a row of white-shirted or business-suited folks who are presumably attorneys, and a sprinkling of spectators, the courtroom is empty. I check my watch — it's nine o'clock exactly. What's going on? I hope Kerry has Plan B ready, because clearly Plan A's been a bust.

Head down, I turn to exit the courtroom . . . and run smack into Remy. I knock his papers out of his hands and three things happen at the same time: he gives a hiss of recognition, his eyes dart to three suntanned, polo-shirted gentlemen sitting halfway down the courtroom, and I hear the bailiff call: "Alyce Trudeau."

It's too much for me. I run headlong from the courtroom, out through the metal detectors and into the summer morning which has turned unaccountably bright and sunny, waving my arms and yelling for Kerry. To her credit, she comes running.

"He's here," I babble. "Remy. Inside Courtroom One. There are three guys that could be the men from LA sitting over on the left. The kids aren't here."

She starts breathing heavily, like a hound on the trail. "Damn the Nautilus PD," she yells, then strips off her gun and handcuffs, handing them to me. "Hold these," she says, and sprints up the steps. I stand there amazed, wondering what I'm supposed to do with these things. Looking around furtively, I stick the gun down the front of my jeans, and put the handcuffs in my back pocket. In a lather of impatience, I wait, pacing one, two, three times around the big planter in the middle of the courtyard, wondering what the hell could be going on inside. And then, improbably, Kerry comes out. With Remy in tow.

"Start the truck," she yells, running, tossing me the keys. I see three guys in polo shirts coming down the stairs maybe twenty yards behind and I race to do as I'm told. Kerry pushes Remy into the front seat of the truck between us, jumps in, and says, "Drive."

I lay rubber away from the courthouse and onto 101 and as I do I glance behind me. There, three unhappy-looking gentlemen in polo shirts are standing beside the planter, looking quite defeated.

Chapter 18

"Turn right here," Kerry says. "I want to get rid of this guy."

"But this'll take us —"

"Around the block to the police station. I know," she says irritably.

I'm too far gone to argue, so I do as she says and find a place in the lot on the other side of the courthouse. "Gimme my cuffs," she tells me and I hand this tough, terse babe her hardware. She grabs Remy by one skinny arm, slaps a cuff on it, and hauls him out of the truck, cuffing his right hand to her left hand. Then she turns to me. "There'll be paper-work," she says. "Maybe go back to the courtroom and see if the kids show up."

"This isn't —" Remy starts and Kerry taps him gently on the nose with the handcuff key.

"Shut up."

To my amazement, he does.

When my knees stop shaking, I lock Kerry's gun in the glove compartment, then walk slowly back to the courtroom. A quick look tells me that, no, the kids haven't appeared, so I dart across the hall to make a phone call.

"Lavner Bay Bed and Breakfast," Eve's cheery voice answers. I'm happy she's at her post but pissed off because she's Eve, so I have a hard time being pleasant.

"It's Allison," I say. "Any calls for me?"

"Not a one," she says. Then, coyly: "You must have been out pretty late last night."

"Yeah. We, you know, looked everyplace we could think of for the kids. Then it got so late that we just stayed at Kerry's." I'm annoyed at myself for thinking I have to explain anything to her.

"Oh, at Kerry's. That must have been nice," she says, and I decide right then and there that I really, truly don't like Eve and that as tempting as the prospect is, I wouldn't sell her my B & B if I were up to my earlobes in red ink. This realization stuns me into silence and Eve hurries on: "There I go again, sticking my nose in your business. I really don't mean to." I can almost hear her smiling.

I ignore her. "If you're okay there I'll just see you later."

"I'm okay here. This is fun, Allison. I can't wait 'til I own a place like this."

"Later, Eve," I tell her wearily, then drag myself back to Courtroom One, taking a seat near the door. To my amazement it's only nine-forty-three. I mean, I feel as though an entire day or maybe a lifetime has passed and I have to force myself to pay attention to the proceedings. Up front, there's a guy I assume is a public defender sitting at the table in conference with an orange-jumpsuited woman in her late twenties — restless brown eyes; lank, dark hair; Minou's little fox face. Alyce Trudeau, I presume. Someone from the DA's office states sternly that the stolen digital camera was worth over $2,000, that the shopkeeper has filed a complaint, that the defendant has no ties to the community and will quite possibly flee, that she has a record of theft in Louisiana, blah, blah, blah. It all turns out much as Kerry predicted it would — no bail. Alyce's court date is set for two weeks from today. Next case. I groan.

Kerry slips into a seat beside me, lips compressed, and hands me a piece of paper. "Phone call for you on my cell phone," she says.

Expecting the troublesome Eve, I look at the number blankly, and then I realize who it belongs to — Ossie's friend Rupert. "It's the kid with the skateboard," I murmur. "Rupert. Maybe the kids are there." Clutching the piece of paper, I hurry from the courtroom and dig in my pocket for a quarter.

This time there's no dumb response. When the phone rings, Rupert's squeaky voice answers at once. "Allison?"

"Yeah. What's up?"

"I, well, you need to know where Ossie is. She

said if she didn't call me by nine-thirty this morning that I was supposed to call you and let you know where she is because she might be in trouble."

"Oh, no. Rupert, where is she?"

"Swimming Cat Cove."

"Swimming Cat . . . I don't get it. Isn't that a story?" I can feel my synapses frying, as I try to make sense of this, and to my relief Kerry appears and takes the phone from me.

"Rupert, you're sure that's what she said? Why did she go there? How long has she — is Minou with her? Okay, thanks."

I'm dazed. "Kerry, what's going on?" Kerry takes my arm and hustles me outside, much the same way she grabbed Remy and marched him along. I don't know about him, but I'm grateful to be hustled. Come to think of it, he probably was, too, given that the choices were jail or the tender mercies of the movie producers.

"She took Minou to the only place she knew of where they'd be absolutely safe. Get in," she says, motioning to the truck and I realize I'm standing like a dope in the parking lot, wringing my hands. I manage to climb into the front seat unaided, and Kerry's tires chirp as she pulls out onto the street.

"Shouldn't we, you know, call the cops?" I ask.

"To hell with that," Kerry says. "You saw how useful they were this morning. Hang on. It's twenty-two miles to Lavner Bay and another nine to the cove. Traffic's pretty light this time of day — we'll be there in thirty minutes max. Put your seat belt on," she tells me, shifting into fourth. We take the corner onto 101 without stopping and I decide the best thing to do is just to pray.

She's as good as her word. Twenty-nine minutes of driving on the right-hand shoulder, passing on hills, and rocketing past RVs have indeed gotten us speedily to Swimming Cat Cove. Which is, as far as I can tell, a wide spot in the road, a grassy meadow, and a cliff.

"C'mon," Kerry says, slamming the truck door and racing to the edge of the precipice. I join her and we look down to the cove below — a tiny, rocky bay about half-filled with churning water. "Shit — the tide's coming in."

"I don't understand," I tell her, kneeling on the grass and looking over the edge. "How can the kids be here? There's no place for them to hide. If there ever was a beach down there, it's covered with water."

"There's a cave," she says, stripping off her jacket. "Ossie found it when we were exploring, when we came to take pictures. It's there, but it's very hard to see. Look down there, about halfway up the cliff right below us — there's a rockfall. And see, there's a little tree growing beside it?"

I'm appalled. "You mean that's where they are? But how do you get to it?"

"From up here."

"You mean they —"

"Climbed down? Yeah. Ossie said she'd done it before."

"Kerry, you mean they're *in there*? In some hole in the cliff?" I'm screaming now not only because I want to but because the surf has really become

172

heavy. A wind has come up and the waves are booming against the side of the cliff with a ferocity I can feel in my feet.

She bends close to me and shouts. "That's what Rupert said. Go get the truck. Back it up to the cliff edge."

I sprint for the truck, back it up toward Kerry, and stop when she raises her hand. She yanks open the driver's side door, hauls out a coil of rope and crawls under the truck where I realize she must be tying the rope to something. Then it occurs to me what she's going to do — she's going to climb down and get the kids.

She throws the other end of the rope over the cliff and it snakes down past the scrubby tree she pointed out, past the rockfall, and lies against the ochre sandstone of the cliff face looking very thin and insubstantial. Then she yanks on a pair of gloves and hurries to the cliff edge, looking at me grimly. I swallow, thinking that she's pretty pale for an Indian. I'm about to make some joke about this when she kneels on the grass, grabs the rope, and lowers herself over the edge.

It's awful because I can't do anything but watch. She's clearly climbed ropes before, because she seems to be lowering herself pretty expertly, but I can't keep from looking at the jagged rocks and roiling water no more than thirty feet below. The tide really is coming in now, filling up the little cove, and every now and then a wind-borne wave reaches a hungry finger up the cliff, reaching for the cave opening, reaching for the scrubby little tree, reaching for Kerry.

Now she's at the tree, which is really no more

173

than an overgrown bush, and she puts her weight on it, testing it, then leans back to look in the cave opening. I don't have a good angle on this since I'm looking down from almost directly above, but it seems to me that a hand emerges from the cave, and then an arm, and then a blonde head. My heart almost stops. Kerry looks up, gives me a thumbs-up sign, and then I see Ossie scuttle out of the cave, grab the little tree, and with Kerry steadying her, begin to climb the rope.

"Ossie, come on!" I call into the racket that the wind and the water is making, urging her to greater speed. As if she's heard me, she looks down once, sees Kerry looking up at us, and climbs faster. When she's close enough, I reach down and haul her up onto the grass beside me and we both look back over the edge.

"Minou's hurt," Ossie yells at me. "She fell when we were climbing down. I think she broke her ankle."

"Can she hang on to Kerry?"

Ossie nods.

Because I can see what Kerry's trying to do — get a good grip on that damned tree so Minou can climb out of the cave and hang onto her. But I don't think it's going to work — the waves are already flinging themselves at Kerry's feet, and any minute now the cave entrance will be flooded. Once that happens, she'll have no choice but to climb up to us and leave Minou in the cave.

Improbably, the wind slackens, and it seems as though the sea takes a breath. The waves, which were dashing themselves against the walls of the cliff, fall silent, still, and I can hear Ossie crying. Kerry looks down, sees her chance, and lets go of the rope with one hand. With the other, she reaches into the cave and drags Minou out. "Now!" I can hear her yell. "Get on my back!"

Minou grabs Kerry's jeans, climbing up her legs and onto her back, where she clings, arms joined around Kerry's neck, face burrowed into her T-shirt. I can almost hear Kerry panting as she rests for a moment, face pressed to the cliff, and I wonder how in hell she's ever going to do it.

"Oh, no," Ossie says, "Look. Out there — the seventh wave."

Sure enough, just offshore, the sea is a washboard of small waves, but there's one that that's gathering force — a tsunami of a wave — and it looks as though it's going to be a killer.

"Climb, Kerry!" we yell, and she steps off the tree. With Minou clinging to her back, she starts up the rope. "C'mon!" we call, pounding our fists on the grass, urging her on, and slowly, ever so slowly, she climbs toward us.

"She's not going to make it!" Ossie screams and I look out past the entrance to the cove and see the seventh wave poised like a hammer to strike the rocks below.

"Yes she is, dammit!" I yell. And then Kerry's gloved hands appear above the edge of the cliff and then her arms and then her head and shoulders. Ossie drags Minou off Kerry's back, and I grab both sleeves of Kerry's T-shirt and hang on as a wave the size of the Nautilus Performing Arts Center hits the cliff and flings itself up the walls and onto the grass, burying us under gallons of eye-stinging salt water and vats of white foam. I feel Kerry losing her grip on the rope, I feel myself sliding toward the edge of the cliff, I feel Kerry's T-shirt slipping through my numbed fingers . . . and then the wave is gone.

"I found a place for my foot," Kerry gasps. "I'm going to take a hitch around my hands with the rope. You'll have to pull me over the edge. I . . . can't climb anymore."

Ossie helps me and together we haul Kerry up and over the edge and onto the grass. Her jeans are shredded at both knees, her nose is bloody where she must have bumped it against the cliff, and she seems unable to let go of the rope. I untangle it from her hands and she rolls over onto her side, looking for the kids.

"They're both here," I tell her. "Everyone's okay."

She buries her head in her arms and for a moment I think she's passed out. But then she raises her head and looks at me. "Guess those hours spent on the rock-climbing wall at REI paid off."

"Guess so."

"Thanks," she says.

"For?"

"For not letting go."

"You're welcome," I tell her, thinking suddenly, painfully, of the B & B and Aunt Grace and Minou and Eve. Not letting go. Okay. Maybe I can live with that.

"C'mon," she says, standing up and grimacing. "Let's get the kids to the hospital in Nautilus. You drive, if you don't mind."

And like a flock of battered seagulls, we limp toward her truck.

Chapter 19

So here we are, sitting in Minou's room at Nautilus General Hospital (she does indeed have a broken ankle) where Ossie and she will share a room until tomorrow when we can take the girls home. They're consuming a carton of chocolate ice cream and giggling. And the cop outside the door (just in case the polo-shirted movie producers do show up) is consuming a cup of coffee and reading a paperback.

"We'll be back tomorrow morning, Ossie," I tell the munchkin.

Her gaze slides over to Minou, then back to me, and I can tell she has a hundred or so questions.

"Tomorrow," I say. "I'm too tired to make sense today."

Kerry winces as we walk down the brightly-lighted hall to the front door. "I haven't had skinned knees for about thirty years," she says. "I'd forgotten how it feels."

"Well, it's never too late to have a happy childhood," I tell her. "That bandage on your nose looks particuarly attractive, too."

In the truck, she slides behind the wheel, groans, then turns to face me. "So what are you going to do?" she asks.

"About?"

"The B & B. You know. Last I heard you were selling out and heading for parts south."

She puts the truck in gear and we turn slowly out onto the street and just as slowly onto 101. I think about my answer as we hit the afternoon traffic snarl at the intersection of Highway 20 and 101, and then head down the little rise onto the bridge that spans the Nautilus bay. Out on the ocean, a late afternoon sun turns the water to cobalt and the sky to periwinkle. Heading for parts south? I don't think so.

"I really don't know about selling," I tell her. "I'm undecided. Besides, my prospective buyer just . . . fell through."

"Hmmm," she says. "Too bad."

"Nah," I tell her. "Aunt Grace wouldn't have liked her."

"Oh," she says. "Why don't you wait and see what happens over the summer. With the Web page and all. And it would be prudent to have something to compare to last year's figures. If business picks up, the place will look even more attractive to a buyer."

"I suppose," I say. "I really need to start thinking about being more businesslike."

"Uh huh," she agrees.

We drive along in companionable silence until we hit Windsock, and then the whole Minou problem comes crashing down on me.

"Minou —" I start.

"Tomorrow," Kerry says. "I'll call my friend at CPS first thing. I'll give her the information I found on the Trudeaus in Minou's home town and she can have her staff try to find the kid's aunt if that's what they decide. We're playing this by the book from now on."

"That sounds good to me."

Now we're pulling into the driveway of the B & B and dammit if I don't feel all warm and smug and proprietary. Kinda like I'm coming home. And (more unlikely still) I find that I'm starting to sniffle. Probably nothing to worry about, I tell myself, drying my eyes on my (well, Kerry's really) salty T-shirt. Just a reaction to almost being pulled into the sea and drowned. Nothing to worry about.

Kerry's out of the truck, leaning on me now, almost asleep on her feet, but we still have to navigate the steps, the porch, and the front door. She moans every step of the way. Inside, at the reception desk, the businesslike Eve is on duty as I knew she would be, not a hair out of place, smile firmly affixed, clothes pressed. She takes one look at the two of us and can only stare.

"Later," I tell her, not giving a damn what she

thinks. but the shock, disapproval, and yes, envy, are plain on her face. "We've had a bad day," I tell her. "A really bad day. So we're going upstairs. To bed. Hold our calls, okay?"

A few of the publications of
THE NAIAD PRESS, INC.
P.O. Box 10543 • Tallahassee, Florida 32302
Phone (904) 539-5965
Toll-Free Order Number: 1-800-533-1973
Mail orders welcome. Please include 15% postage.
Write or call for our free catalog which also features an
incredible selection of lesbian videos.

SWIMMING CAT COVE by Lauren Douglas. 192 pp. 2nd
Allison O'Neil Mystery.   ISBN 1-56280-168-6 $11.95

THE LOVING LESBIAN by Claire McNab and Sharon Gedan.
240 pp. Explore the experiences that make lesbian love unique.
                                                  ISBN 1-56280-169-4   14.95

COURTED by Celia Cohen. 160 pp. Sparkling romantic
encounter.   ISBN 1-56280-166-X   11.95

SEASONS OF THE HEART by Jackie Calhoun. 240 pp. Romance
through the years.   ISBN 1-56280-167-8   11.95

K. C. BOMBER by Janet McClellan. 208 pp. 1st Tru North
mystery.   ISBN 1-56280-157-0   11.95

LAST RITES by Tracey Richardson. 192 pp. 1st Stevie Houston
mystery.   ISBN 1-56280-164-3   11.95

EMBRACE IN MOTION by Karin Kallmaker. 256 pp. A whirlwind
love affair.   ISBN 1-56280-165-1   11.95

HOT CHECK by Peggy J. Herring. 192 pp. Will workaholic Alice
fall for guitarist Ricky?   ISBN 1-56280-163-5   11.95

OLD TIES by Saxon Bennett. 176 pp. Can Cleo surrender to a
passionate new love?   ISBN 1-56280-159-7   11.95

LOVE ON THE LINE by Laura DeHart Young. 176 pp. Will Stef win Kay's
heart?   ISBN 1-56280-162-7 $11.95

DEVIL'S LEG CROSSING by Kaye Davis. 192 pp. 1st Maris Middleton
mystery.   ISBN 1-56280-158-9   11.95

COSTA BRAVA by Marta Balletbo Coll. 144 pp. Read the book,
see the movie!   ISBN 1-56280-153-8   11.95

MEETING MAGDALENE & OTHER STORIES by
Marilyn Freeman. 144 pp. Read the book, see the movie!
                                                  ISBN 1-56280-170-8   11.95

SECOND FIDDLE by Kate Calloway. 208 pp. P.I. Cassidy James'
second case.   ISBN 1-56280-169-6   11.95

LAUREL by Isabel Miller. 128 pp. By the author of the beloved
Patience and Sarah.   ISBN 1-56280-146-5   10.95

LOVE OR MONEY by Jackie Calhoun. 240 pp. The romance of
real life.   ISBN 1-56280-147-3   10.95

SMOKE AND MIRRORS by Pat Welch. 224 pp. 5th Helen Black
Mystery.   ISBN 1-56280-143-0   10.95

DANCING IN THE DARK edited by Barbara Grier & Christine
Cassidy. 272 pp. Erotic love stories by Naiad Press authors.
                                         ISBN 1-56280-144-9   14.95

TIME AND TIME AGAIN by Catherine Ennis. 176 pp. Passionate
love affair.   ISBN 1-56280-145-7   10.95

PAXTON COURT by Diane Salvatore. 256 pp. Erotic and wickedly
funny contemporary tale about the business of learning to live
together.   ISBN 1-56280-114-7   10.95

INNER CIRCLE by Claire McNab. 208 pp. 8th Carol Ashton
Mystery.   ISBN 1-56280-135-X   10.95

LESBIAN SEX: AN ORAL HISTORY by Susan Johnson.
240 pp. Need we say more?   ISBN 1-56280-142-2   14.95

BABY, IT'S COLD by Jaye Maiman. 256 pp. 5th Robin Miller
Mystery.   ISBN 1-56280-141-4   19.95

WILD THINGS by Karin Kallmaker. 240 pp. By the undisputed
mistress of lesbian romance.   ISBN 1-56280-139-2   10.95

THE GIRL NEXT DOOR by Mindy Kaplan. 208 pp. Just what
you'd expect.   ISBN 1-56280-140-6   11.95

NOW AND THEN by Penny Hayes. 240 pp. Romance on the
westward journey.   ISBN 1-56280-121-X   11.95

HEART ON FIRE by Diana Simmonds. 176 pp. The romantic and
erotic rival of *Curious Wine.*   ISBN 1-56280-152-X   11.95

DEATH AT LAVENDER BAY by Lauren Wright Douglas. 208 pp.
1st Allison O'Neil Mystery.   ISBN 1-56280-085-X   11.95

YES I SAID YES I WILL by Judith McDaniel. 272 pp. Hot
romance by famous author.   ISBN 1-56280-138-4   11.95

FORBIDDEN FIRES by Margaret C. Anderson. Edited by Mathilda
Hills. 176 pp. Famous author's "unpublished" Lesbian romance.
                                         ISBN 1-56280-123-6   21.95

SIDE TRACKS by Teresa Stores. 160 pp. Gender-bending
Lesbians on the road.   ISBN 1-56280-122-8   10.95

HOODED MURDER by Annette Van Dyke. 176 pp. 1st Jessie
Batelle Mystery.   ISBN 1-56280-134-1   10.95

WILDWOOD FLOWERS by Julia Watts. 208 pp. Hilarious and
heart-warming tale of true love.   ISBN 1-56280-127-9   10.95

NEVER SAY NEVER by Linda Hill. 224 pp. Rule #1: Never get involved with . . . ISBN 1-56280-126-0 10.95

THE SEARCH by Melanie McAllester. 240 pp. Exciting top cop Tenny Mendoza case. ISBN 1-56280-150-3 10.95

THE WISH LIST by Saxon Bennett. 192 pp. Romance through the years. ISBN 1-56280-125-2 10.95

FIRST IMPRESSIONS by Kate Calloway. 208 pp. P.I. Cassidy James' first case. ISBN 1-56280-133-3 10.95

OUT OF THE NIGHT by Kris Bruyer. 192 pp. Spine-tingling thriller. ISBN 1-56280-120-1 10.95

NORTHERN BLUE by Tracey Richardson. 224 pp. Police recruits Miki & Miranda — passion in the line of fire. ISBN 1-56280-118-X 10.95

LOVE'S HARVEST by Peggy J. Herring. 176 pp. by the author of *Once More With Feeling*. ISBN 1-56280-117-1 10.95

THE COLOR OF WINTER by Lisa Shapiro. 208 pp. Romantic love beyond your wildest dreams. ISBN 1-56280-116-3 10.95

FAMILY SECRETS by Laura DeHart Young. 208 pp. Enthralling romance and suspense. ISBN 1-56280-119-8 10.95

INLAND PASSAGE by Jane Rule. 288 pp. Tales exploring conventional & unconventional relationships. ISBN 0-930044-56-8 10.95

DOUBLE BLUFF by Claire McNab. 208 pp. 7th Carol Ashton Mystery. ISBN 1-56280-096-5 10.95

BAR GIRLS by Lauran Hoffman. 176 pp. See the movie, read the book! ISBN 1-56280-115-5 10.95

THE FIRST TIME EVER edited by Barbara Grier & Christine Cassidy. 272 pp. Love stories by Naiad Press authors. ISBN 1-56280-086-8 14.95

MISS PETTIBONE AND MISS McGRAW by Brenda Weathers. 208 pp. A charming ghostly love story. ISBN 1-56280-151-1 10.95

CHANGES by Jackie Calhoun. 208 pp. Involved romance and relationships. ISBN 1-56280-083-3 10.95

FAIR PLAY by Rose Beecham. 256 pp. 3rd Amanda Valentine Mystery. ISBN 1-56280-081-7 10.95

PAYBACK by Celia Cohen. 176 pp. A gripping thriller of romance, revenge and betrayal. ISBN 1-56280-084-1 10.95

THE BEACH AFFAIR by Barbara Johnson. 224 pp. Sizzling summer romance/mystery/intrigue. ISBN 1-56280-090-6 10.95

GETTING THERE by Robbi Sommers. 192 pp. Nobody does it like Robbi! ISBN 1-56280-099-X 10.95

FINAL CUT by Lisa Haddock. 208 pp. 2nd Carmen Ramirez Mystery. ISBN 1-56280-088-4 10.95

FLASHPOINT by Katherine V. Forrest. 256 pp. A Lesbian
blockbuster! ISBN 1-56280-079-5   11.95

CLAIRE OF THE MOON by Nicole Conn. Audio Book —Read
by Marianne Hyatt. ISBN 1-56280-113-9   16.95

FOR LOVE AND FOR LIFE: INTIMATE PORTRAITS OF
LESBIAN COUPLES by Susan Johnson. 224 pp.
ISBN 1-56280-091-4   14.95

DEVOTION by Mindy Kaplan. 192 pp. See the movie — read
the book! ISBN 1-56280-093-0   10.95

SOMEONE TO WATCH by Jaye Maiman. 272 pp. 4th Robin
Miller Mystery. ISBN 1-56280-095-7   10.95

GREENER THAN GRASS by Jennifer Fulton. 208 pp. A young
woman — a stranger in her bed. ISBN 1-56280-092-2   10.95

TRAVELS WITH DIANA HUNTER by Regine Sands. Erotic
lesbian romp. Audio Book (2 cassettes) ISBN 1-56280-107-4   16.95

CABIN FEVER by Carol Schmidt. 256 pp. Sizzling suspense
and passion. ISBN 1-56280-089-1   10.95

THERE WILL BE NO GOODBYES by Laura DeHart Young. 192
pp. Romantic love, strength, and friendship. ISBN 1-56280-103-1   10.95

FAULTLINE by Sheila Ortiz Taylor. 144 pp. Joyous comic
lesbian novel. ISBN 1-56280-108-2   9.95

OPEN HOUSE by Pat Welch. 176 pp. 4th Helen Black Mystery.
ISBN 1-56280-102-3   10.95

ONCE MORE WITH FEELING by Peggy J. Herring. 240 pp.
Lighthearted, loving romantic adventure. ISBN 1-56280-089-2   11.95

FOREVER by Evelyn Kennedy. 224 pp. Passionate romance — love
overcoming all obstacles. ISBN 1-56280-094-9   10.95

WHISPERS by Kris Bruyer. 176 pp. Romantic ghost story
ISBN 1-56280-082-5   10.95

NIGHT SONGS by Penny Mickelbury. 224 pp. 2nd Gianna Maglione
Mystery. ISBN 1-56280-097-3   10.95

GETTING TO THE POINT by Teresa Stores. 256 pp. Classic
southern Lesbian novel. ISBN 1-56280-100-7   10.95

These are just a few of the many Naiad Press titles — we are the oldest and
largest lesbian/feminist publishing company in the world. We also offer an
enormous selection of lesbian video products. Please request a complete
catalog. We offer personal service; we encourage and welcome direct mail
orders from individuals who have limited access to bookstores carrying our
publications.